KT-469-313

Nathalia BUTTFACE

and the MOST ~~Embarrassing~~ five minutes of Fame EVER

BY
Nigel Smith

Illustrated by
Sarah Horne

HarperCollins *Children's Books*

First published in Great Britain by HarperCollins Children's Books in 2015
HarperCollins Children's Books is a division of HarperCollins*Publishers* Ltd,
HarperCollins *Publishers*, 1 London Bridge Street, London SE1 9GF

The HarperCollins Children's Books website address is
www.harpercollins.co.uk

1

Nathalia Buttface and the Most Embarrassing
Five Minutes of Fame Ever

ISBN 978-0-00-754525-4

Printed and bound in England by
Clays Ltd, St Ives plc

Nathalia BUTTFACE

NIGEL SMITH has been a journalist, busker, TV
comedy producer and script writer, winning
an award for his BBC 4 radio comedy, *Vent*,
based on his own life-threatening brain illness.
More importantly, he has been – and still is – an
embarrassing dad. Much like Nathalia Buttface,
his three children are continually mortified by
his ill-advised trousers, comedic hats,
low-quality jokes, poorly chosen motor vehicles,
unique sense of direction and unfortunate
ukulele playing. Unlike his hero, Ivor Bumolé,
he doesn't write Christmas cracker
jokes for a living. Yet.

This is Nigel's third book about
Nathalia Buttface.

C016078333

Check out these great reviews from Lovereading4kids:

"Without a doubt the funniest book I have ever read." *Sam, age 10*

"The plot was hilarious and the ending was brilliant and unexpected." *Eloise Mae, age 11*

"This book made me laugh out loud many times and I didn't want it to end." *Lily, age 9*

"I rate this book five stars because it is so funny and really cool." *Jenny, age 8*

"This book is hilarious, amazing and gives me an embarrassing feeling on behalf of Nathalia!" *Elspeth, age 9*

"Nathalia Bumolé is one of the unluckiest kids ever, and most of it is her dad's fault!" *Elise Marie, age 9 ½*

"Makes me glad my dad is nothing like this dad, although he is still very embarrassing." *Emma, age 7*

To Carole, because without her I'd just be an embarrassing dad without a book.

And thank you to Nicola, because without her I wouldn't have a title for this book. Which would be embarrassing.

CHAPTER ONE

····

"ARE YOU SURE NO ONE ELSE IS GOING TO see this video?" asked Penny Posnitch doubtfully.

"I'm not an idiot," said Nat. "I'm not my dad."

"Will you hurry up? My arms are getting tired," complained Darius.

"Just hold the camera straight and press the record button when I tell you," snapped Nat.

The three of them were in Nat's back garden. It was a lovely warm afternoon at the end of the school holidays. The sun was shining, the flowers were out, Dad was upstairs trying to write Christmas cracker jokes and shouting rude words at his laptop, and the three friends were making a dance video.

The dance video was going very badly.

And so was Dad's joke writing; every so often they would hear him yell: "Oh heck, that's not funny. I'm doomed…"

"I wonder if he needs a hand," said Darius, putting the camera down. "I've got a great joke about a monkey who needs to go to the toilet."

"The 'monkey who needs to go to the toilet' joke is not a joke anyone wants in their cracker while they're eating their Christmas pudding," said Nat. "Can we please do our dance video?"

"I want to hear the monkey joke," said Penny.

Nat started hopping up and down. "I've been trying to make this video all morning," she shouted. "Will you both CONCENTRATE."

"I only came round to show Nathalia the new Dinky Blue, Girl Guru episode online," grumbled Penny. "And now I've been roped into this."

"She's rubbish," said Darius, making sick noises. "You should watch Doom Ninja Pete instead. He blew up a pig last week."

"That's disgusting," said Penny, who was an animal lover.

Darius started doing his impression of a pig blowing up in slow motion, until Nat ran over and started throttling him.

"Pick-up-the-camera-and-film-us-doing-the-dance…"

"OK," he squawked.

"Play the song on the phone, Penny."

"I can't remember the dance move after the song goes: 'Baby baby oooh baby'," said Penny.

"Which 'Baby baby oooh baby'?" asked Nat. "She sings 'Baby baby oooh baby' about a ZILLION times. The song is CALLED 'Baby baby oooh baby'."

"Er – the first time," said Penny.

"That's the START of the song," shouted Nat

in frustration. "I've shown you the moves about a thousand million billion times at least and I'm not even exaggerating. What is the matter with you? It's step left, arms cross, turn, arms up, bend, slide and wiggle. Got it?"

"You're not a very good dance teacher," said Penny sulkily. "You're always shouting."

"That's how good dance teachers teach dance," shouted Nat.

"Do you want me to film this bit?" asked Darius, filming that bit.

"Of course I don't want you to film this bit; stop filming this bit," said Nat.

"When I saw Flora Marling's dance video there was no one shouting," grumbled Penny.

"That's because Flora Marling is flipping perfect, we all know that," said Nat. "So this dance video has to be better than perfect."

"You can't be better than perfect," corrected Darius, who was filming with one hand while picking his nose with the other.

"I'm not doing anything while he's doing

THAT," said Penny, pulling a face.

Eventually Nat got Penny to concentrate and Darius to wash his hands and after a few more shouty rehearsals, she and Penny were doing the dance.

Nat was especially proud of a new move she had invented called the Prancing Pony. It was super-tricky and Penny had already got it wrong once and ended up in a hedge.

But finally it was going well.

"...Up and hop and jump and slide and hop," whispered Nat, reminding Penny what to do, as they reached the tricky bit. To her delight Penny was doing it BETTER THAN PERFECTLY when...

"I've gotta go," said Darius, putting the camera down on the ground. "See you."

"WHAT? We haven't finished, you total chimp," said Nat.

"Then you shouldn't have taken so long, Buttface," said Darius. "I'm busy."

"Doing what? Where are you going?" Nat

asked, infuriated, but she didn't get an answer because at that moment Dad appeared from the house.

"Just thought I'd see if you were OK," he said. "I was watching you jiggle about and it looked like you'd swallowed space hoppers."

"THAT'S IT!" yelled Nat, throwing herself on the grass. "I can't work like this."

"Ooh, you taking selfies?" said Dad, picking up the camera. "Urgh, why's this camera all sticky?" Darius, standing by the back gate, grinned.

"We are NOT taking selfies," said Nat. "And I don't even know how you know about selfies, you're so old."

"What are you up to then?" said Dad, adding jokingly, "I hope you're not thinking of putting anything on to the online inter cyber-space web."

Nat hadn't been intending to put her dance video online, but she didn't want to be told she COULDN'T.

"Can if I want," she said. She wasn't usually

this rude, but was hot and tired and frustrated and scratchy.

"Stop showing off in front of your friends," said Dad gently, which was one of the MOST ANNOYING THINGS HE COULD SAY. It was up there with:

You're only grumpy because you're tired.

You're only grumpy because you're hungry.

You're only grumpy because you've found Nan's false teeth in the biscuit tin again. AFTER you've eaten a digestive.

"I am NOT showing off, baldy," said Nat, showing off, "but if I wanted to, I could put this dance routine online and get a million hits and make us rich and famous and THEN you'd be sorry."

"You're very grumpy," said Dad. "You must be tired. Or possibly hungry. Or have you been in the biscuit tin?"

"You said you wouldn't put this video online," hissed Penny. "I don't want anyone else to see it. You promised."

"I'm not saying I'm GOING to put it online, I'm just saying I COULD," said Nat stubbornly.

"Online is a very dangerous place," said Dad, patiently. "Do you remember when you and Daddy had that talk and Daddy said it was like a big nasty dark cave with monsters in it and you said it sounded very scary and you promised to stay outside the cave forever and ever?"

"Yes, when I was SIX, Dad," shouted Nat. Penny sniggered. Nat felt herself getting red in the face.

"Every flipping day," she yelled, waving her arms about like mad, "you always EMBARRASS me. People are watching, Dad. Can't you be NORMAL?"

She did one last furious high hop, but landed awkwardly on a damp patch of grass.

Her feet shot out from under her, her legs went straight up in the air and she landed heavily on something. Something alive.

There was a pause. Then a look of horror. Then she yelled:

"AAAAAARRRRRRGGGGH!"

There was something buzzing in her pants! It was as cross as any bee could be. Especially a bee that had then been happily slurping pollen off a flower when it was rudely sat on.

Nat ran around the garden smacking herself on the bum like she was trying to ride herself to victory in the Grand National. Finally, inevitably, she felt the sting.

"OOOOOH!" she yelled in pain. "EEEEEE!"

With that she dashed out of the garden.

And into... fame.

CHAPTER TWO

• • • •

NAT DIDN'T BECOME FAMOUS IMMEDIATELY—no, it took her the whole weekend.

And of course it took the power of what Dad annoyingly called the 'inter cyber-space web' to do it.

Nat was blissfully unaware of the fuss she was causing online. This was because, for a start, she had no idea that a video of herself WAS online. But, as it turned out, it was, and it was getting *more* online by the minute. People *like* sharing. And they especially like sharing funny videos of furious girls running around gardens shouting: "Can't you be *normal* – aaaarrrgh, ooooh, eeeee!"

All it needed was someone to put it online in the first place...

Then, over the next couple of days, while her video was being chuckled over by more and more people, Nathalia was actually totally OFFLINE. Mum had just come home after two weeks working abroad so Nat had *loads* of catching-up with her to do. She never even noticed when the battery on her mobile phone ran out.

And so she missed A LOT of texts from her classmates. Which was even worse than it sounds, because Nat was always *desperate* to get texts from her classmates. No one ever texted her. Nat had given her mobile number to literally EVERYONE she knew, but the only messages she ever received were from the phone company, trying to sell her a new phone.

But now, waiting for her in the cyber-darkness, were loads of them.

Texts like:

OMG!!! LOL. ROFL.

And

YOU ARE SOOOOO FUNNY.

And

HAVE YOU SEEN YOURSELF??????

And

U. R. A ★

Meanwhile, most of Nat's catching-up with Mum was spent clothes shopping while telling Mum how utterly rubbish Dad had been recently.

The Atomic Dustbin – Dad's horrible old camper van – had broken down twice picking her up from school and once when he'd volunteered to take the hockey team to an away match.

"We were so late the other team was allowed to start without us and we were ten-nil down before we even got on the pitch," she complained, making Mum giggle.

Then she revealed Dad had made them pork pie and chips for tea THREE times last week. And it would have been four times but Bad News Nan had come round, insisted they had a proper meal with vitamins, and then ordered pizzas because cheese counted as veg, near enough.

Mum's shoulders shook with laughter as they picked out tops.

"He does look after you pretty well though," chuckled Mum in the changing rooms. "I mean, compared to being looked after by a trained gorilla."

"Why are those girls staring at me?" said Nat, noticing a gaggle of gigglers, pointing and sniggering in the shop doorway. "Are my pants showing?"

Mum came out of the changing room and raised her eyebrows at the girls, who took the hint and ran off. Nat LOVED the way Mum could do that. She had seen Mum reduce grown men to quivering jelly by the simple raising of her fearsome eyebrows. Including the policemen who were always telling her off for driving much too fast in her little red car.

Dad couldn't scare anybody, thought Nat. *He only makes people laugh, the big dope. Even when he's TRYING to be fearsome.*

Nat sometimes practised raising her eyebrows at Darius when he was being especially annoying, but he just laughed and said it made her look cross-eyed.

"Can't you be NORMAL?" shouted one of the girls outside, and the others shrieked with laughter as they took off through the shopping centre, smacking themselves on the bum.

What a weird bunch of girls, thought Nat, but within five seconds she had forgotten all about them because Mum said she'd buy her a new pair of flip-flops.

But a similarly strange thing happened as they were choosing a DVD to watch that night. Nat was having a good-natured argument with Mum as to whether they watch a big disaster movie (Mum's choice) or a film about girls who win a singing competition and sing a lot (Nat's choice). Dad wasn't there; he was just going to have to watch what he was told.

Nat suddenly became aware of a couple of

boys over by the comic book films who were sniggering and looking over at her. She glared at them and they slunk off.

"People are watching," one said, for no apparent reason, then fell about laughing.

But yet again, Nat soon forgot all about it when Mum suggested they could go to the shop that sold bath bombs next.

It was only late on Sunday night, in bed, snuggled in and smelling of crème-brûlée bath bomb, that Nat plugged her phone in and was instantly greeted by a million pings that told her SHE HAD MESSAGES.

I'm popular! she thought. *I'm finally popular! Go me.*

But then... she read them.

"What have you done you've ruined my life I can't bear to look I'm going to kill you and I'm not even joking," yelled Nat, thundering down the stairs in search of Dad.

Dad was sitting on the sofa with Mum, just

about to pour himself a glass of wine. When he saw the furious expression on Nat's face, he poured a very big one.

"Shouldn't you be in bed, love?" he said nervously, seeing his doom approaching in the shape of a twelve-year-old in a purple tiger-striped onesie.

Nat waved her phone under his nose.

"You've done something stupid and horrible and embarrassing, haven't you, Dad?"

Dad coughed and fidgeted. Next to him, Mum was starting to raise her eyebrows.

"Is this about the funny video by any chance?" he asked, trying to sound as if he wasn't actually IN MASSIVE TROUBLE.

"What video is this, Ivor?" asked Mum, quietly. There was only one thing scarier than Mum shouting, and that was Mum being quiet.

"Ah yes, it's probably easier if I show you…" began Dad, with a nervous chuckle. He picked up his laptop from the floor and opened it. It shone into life.

"Do you like my new screensaver?" he asked, trying to change the subject. "It's us at Legoland just before I knocked over Big Ben and got banned for life."

"I DON'T CARE – WHAT DID YOU DO?"

"I made myself a website," announced Dad, clicking the keys. "I'm taking Christmas crackers into the twenty-first century."

On the screen, a cartoon cracker snapped open and out fluttered a joke.

"That's the joke about the monkey needing the toilet," gasped Nat. "Which means Darius flipping Bagley made this website for you. I knew YOU couldn't do it. You don't know anything about computers."

"I do," said Dad defensively. "I designed the whole thing."

"Where's this video?" snapped Mum. Dad moved the mouse over to a drawing of a large pile of rubbish.

"It's here in this area called *The Jokeheap*," explained Dad excitedly. "I can put all sorts of funny things here. Darius showed me how. It's like my comedy scrapbook."

"Or a dump," offered Mum, "where visitors can rummage about in the rubbish of your mind."

Dad clicked a bit more and fresh images rose from the rubble.

"Look, I put a video of a dog who sings the national anthem in there, and the one where that boy tries to skateboard on ice. And, um—"

"AND THE VIDEO OF ME DANCING AND SHOUTING AT YOU!" shrieked Nat in horror as her face rose up from the jokey rubbish dump.

"Oh no, not all of it," corrected Dad. "Only the funny bits. Which is mostly you jumping up and down and shouting – in a cute way, obviously."

"People are watching…" said Video Nat, "… can't you be normal?"

A memory struggled to the surface of Nat's brain as Video Nat ran around smacking herself and making silly noises. Why were those words so familiar?

"You're making a mountain out of a molehill," said Dad. "I'll take it down. Anyway, not many people will have seen it yet. Look here, I've got a counter on my website. It shows I've only had ten hits. And five of those were *me*, checking on how many hits I had."

Mum put her head in her hands. "It only takes one person to see it and share it," she said. Dad looked blank. Mum pushed him off the laptop and tapped some keys.

"Look," she said. "Here in the comments bit."

"I never read the comments," admitted Dad, "because people can be very rude about my jokes."

"Shut up and listen," said Mum. "There's a comment from 'CatLover 34543' who says:

All the jokes here are rubbish, but I love the video of the funny little 'Can't you be normal' girl. I'm sharing this with EVERYONE I know. And I know loads of people.

"No problemo, I'll just email her and ask her

to delete it," said Dad. "She seems like a nice person. She loves cats."

"Don't you know ANYTHING, Dad?" said Nat. "I *had* this talk with you about online safety, didn't I?"

"Umm..." said Dad.

"Tell him, Mum," said Nat, throwing her arms up in despair.

"Once something is on the Internet, it's ALWAYS THERE," said Mum, as if she was explaining something to a small and particularly dense child. "Surely even you can remember that?"

"And now loads of people have copied the video and shared it all over town," said Nat. Suddenly, with a sick horror, she realised where she had heard those words. In the shopping centre. From COMPLETE STRANGERS. That video must have spread far and wide.

"I'm doomed. I can never go out again!" she said tearfully. "And yes, Dad, you ARE a complete idiot."

CHAPTER THREE

· · · ·

OF COURSE, NAT KNEW SHE WOULD HAVE TO LEAVE the house again. But she was determined to put it off for as long as possible. There was one more week of holidays left and she spent most of it sulking at home. NOW she was getting plenty of texts; she just didn't want to read them. She prayed this would all be over and forgotten about by the time school started again.

"Stop hiding in your room," said Bad News Nan one morning, popping her head round the bedroom door and scattering biscuit crumbs as she spoke. "You'll get rickets without enough sunlight. Terrible, is rickets. You get horrible bendy legs. Doctors thought I had it once, but turns out my stockings were too tight."

Nat wriggled further under the covers.

Bad News Nan sat heavily on the bed and looked around for something to munch. When she couldn't see anything, she put her false teeth back in her pocket, as she only ever used them for eating.

The dog, who was hiding with Nat, emerged from under the bed and started nibbling at Nan's trouser pocket. He loved sucking her false teeth. They were so tasty.

Nat peeked out from under the covers. The dog with

Nan's teeth WAS hilarious, after all.

"You had a great-auntie who suffered with her nerves," Bad News Nan droned on, not noticing the snuffling dog. "Great-auntie Primula. She took to her bed one Christmas after her pudding set fire to the living-room curtains. Refused to move out of her room again, even when she got the boils."

"Boils?" asked Nat, interested.

"Pustules, really. Oooh they were big enough to make the doctors weep," said Bad News Nan with relish. "Record-breaking, they were. She made the local papers with them. People felt sorry for her, but not me. I think she just liked the attention."

Nat wasn't sure that anyone would want to be famous for having pustules, but she didn't want Nan to think *she* was trying to get attention. She was in bed trying to AVOID attention.

"I'm getting up now, Nan," she said, just as the dog made a grab for the gnashers. He ran off with them clattering around in his mouth. Nan said a rude word and leapt up as quickly as she could, which wasn't very quickly, and the pair of them thudded down the stairs.

It's not fair, thought Nat, getting dressed. *I'm way less bonkers than anyone else in this family, and it's ME people are laughing at...*

When Nat at last emerged from her room, she was persuaded to go shopping with Mum and Bad News Nan. Mum wanted to buy vegetables, because Dad never bought any apart from potatoes, and Bad News Nan needed some ointment. When Nat asked why she needed the ointment, Nan told her. And then Nat felt a bit sick and wished she hadn't.

In the shopping centre, Nat pulled the strings on her hoodie's hood so tight around her face that she kept bumping into things. They went to their favourite caff and the only thing she would have was a milkshake, which she could drink by poking a straw through the tiny hole in her hood.

It was miserable, trying to avoid being laughed at. Mum kept reassuring her that people would forget about the video and move on to the next funny thing.

But as days went by, Nat's angry outburst got more and more popular, and more and more shared. Like a snowball rolling down a massive mountain, gathering millions of snowflakes and turning into a horrible avalanche of frosty doom, EVERYONE was finding the clip hilarious and passing it on to their friends.

Perhaps it was Nat's face, her wild flying hair, her little wiggly dance of outrage, her hoppy, bum-slapping dance, but *something* made people love it. And worst of all, she had come up with a phrase that people just liked using.

On Monday she heard the window cleaner over the road shout to his lad with the bucket: "Stop whistling. People are watching. Can't you be normal?"

On Tuesday, Nat heard annoying local morning radio DJ Cabbage burble: "We've got a caller who says she's just seen Prince Charles doing a hot wash down the launderette. All I can say to her is: 'Doris, can't you be normal?'"

On Wednesday Nat saw a comedian on the telly make fun of someone in the audience who was wearing an unfortunate pink tank top. "Why did you put that on?" he mocked. "People are watching…" The audience had started laughing even before he finished with…

"…Can't you be normal?"

Nat immediately turned over to watch a documentary about a lost tribe in the Amazon. But even then she was half expecting one of the tribe to interrupt a war dance with: "Stop that, Dave, there's a film crew. People are watching. Can't you be normal?"

On Thursday, chat show host Dilbert Starburst said it about ten times all through his show and it got bigger laughs every flipping time.

And finally on Friday even the Prime Minister joined in the fun. He was teasing a politician from a foreign country at a big meeting. "Calm down, dear," he said, in his usual smug voice, "people are watching. Can't you be NORMAL?"

"Of course she can't be normal," muttered one of the Prime Minister's crawly bum-lick friends, "she's from Belgium."

Oh great, so I can never go to Belgium now, thought Nat, watching the news. *I bet the whole country will blame me for that comment.*

Naturally Nat made Dad suffer for his online crimes. She couldn't decide between shouting at him continually or refusing to talk to him, so she opted for a mixture of both, depending on whether she wanted him to make her a bacon sandwich, for example.

"Come on, love, you know I hate it when you're cross with me," he said on Saturday lunchtime as she tucked into one of his big, greasy, delicious bacon sandwiches.

"Which is odd, because you make her cross a lot," said Mum, who had been NO HELP TO DAD all week.

"Well, you can stop being cross because I've found out how to make it all better," said Dad, looking quite pleased with himself.

"You CAN'T make it better," said Nat, who was actually starting to feel less cross with him and more sorry for herself. Besides, she had to admit Dad did make excellent bacon sandwiches. "It's not a grazed knee that you can kiss better and put a plaster on."

She was only using that as an example, but Dad suddenly looked guilty. "I've apologised for getting you stuck in that babies' swing a thousand times," he said, remembering a time when she had grazed her knee. "I thought you were too little for the big swings."

"I haven't heard this story," said Mum quietly.

"Now be fair, Nat," said Dad, very very

quickly, "you only grazed your knee when the fireman who cut you out of the swing dropped you on the gravel. Technically that wasn't my fault."

He jumped up out of arm's reach and plopped more bacon in the pan. Then he said, "Now who wants to hear about the *brilliant* thing Dad's just done?"

"There is NOTHING you can say to make this situation better," said Nat firmly, "except that we're emigrating. At the very least I'll have to change schools. Everyone used to make fun of me – mostly thanks to you, Dad – and it's taken me ages to go from being laughed at to just being ignored. I was hoping this might be the term where I got popular. But no, I'm going to be back down in the 'getting laughed at' spot again."

"Would a hundred pounds make you feel any better?" asked Dad, over the sound of sizzling bacon.

"Ivor, you can't just give her a hundred pounds to make her stop shouting at you," said

Mum. "That's a terrible idea, even for you."

"It's not FROM me," said Dad, smiling, "it's from the hair salon in town. They saw you doing that thing I'm not going to say because I don't want to be shouted at again, and they want you to be a model for them, and it's all thanks to Dad!"

"What if she doesn't WANT to be a model?" asked Mum. "My little girl doesn't need a load of people telling her how pretty and wonderful and beautiful she is, and giving her money just for being gorgeous, do you, Nat?"

There was a long pause, when all that could be heard was the sizzle of the smoky pan.

"Yeah, that sounds horrible," said Nat slowly, thinking that it sounded rather nice, on the whole. "Although... maybe I should let poor old Dad try and make it up to me. It'll make him feel better."

Dad smiled. "They recognised you from the – the – you know, the *thing*, and left a message on the website saying that you were the perfect girl to advertise their new styling gel."

"I'm not saying yes," said Nat, "but is it cash and what do I have to do?"

Mum looked at the two of them. "You're both as bad as each other," she said with a sigh.

"Dad doesn't get EVERYTHING wrong," said Nat.

Then the smoke alarm went off as Dad set the pan on fire.

CHAPTER FOUR

• • • •

"You do look funny with all your eyebrows burned off," chuckled Nat as they reached the hair salon. "Maybe you should get one of the ladies in here to draw some on for you? Loads of people do it."

"No, loads of *women* do it," corrected Dad.

"Or maybe they can stick some real hair on from all the clippings," giggled Nat. "There's tons on the floor – black ones, blonde ones, curly—"

"If you don't mention it, no one will notice,"

said Dad.

"Rubbish," laughed Nat as they went inside the shop. "The only reason no one's pointed and laughed at *me* today is because they're all pointing and laughing at *you*."

"Glad to help," said Dad with a fixed smile.

The salon was called THE FINAL CUT and was decorated with pictures of movie stars.

"Why's it called 'The Final Cut'?" asked Dad when he met the manager. "You've changed the name. It used to be 'Curl up and Dye'."

"Yes, we thought it would give us a more Hollywood Image," said the manager, who was called Irene Hideous and had leathery orange skin and severe, short blonde hair. "You know, like they say 'cut' when they make films."

"Yes, but 'The *Final* Cut' sounds more like someone having their head chopped off," said Dad brightly. "Get it?"

There was a horrible pause.

"I hadn't thought of that," said Irene Hideous. "That sign cost us a fortune, and so did all those pictures. I'm not changing it again so please don't tell my customers that."

Nat sighed.

"You could do a Halloween theme though," continued Dad, enthusiastic and embarrassing as ever. "You could have a big chopping block over there and customers could put their head on it and you could cut their hair while you ask them if they've got any last requests."

"Last requests?" said a very old lady who had just come out from under a dryer. Her hair was bright blue. "My last request is to have my ashes put in a big egg timer. I do like to be useful. Even though nobody notices."

"Shut up, Mum," said another elderly woman sitting next to her.

"Besides," continued the very old lady, "my daughter here hasn't managed to boil me a decent egg for sixty years."

"If that's the way you feel about it, you can pay for your own hairdo," said her daughter, storming out.

Irene Hideous looked at Dad venomously.

"Now she's gone I can tell you my REAL last request," cackled the old lady. She then said something SO RUDE that Nat thought her ears were going to fall off.

Quickly the manager ushered Nat and Dad into the back of the salon, next to the sinks.

"RIGHT, well, we're trying to attract younger customers," explained Mrs Hideous, "so we thought the 'Can't you be normal' girl—"

"My name's Nathalia," said Nat.

"Yes, you, apparently you're a new celebrity that is popular with youngsters. You're not even that bad-looking," said Mrs Hideous as she grabbed Nat's face and started pulling the skin around. "There are cheekbones in there, somewhere."

This isn't like being a model in the way Mum said, thought Nat as her face was squished. She quite liked being called a 'celebrity' though.

Irene Hideous ran her long, bony orange fingers through Nat's hair, sizing it up expertly.

"Oh dear," she said. "It's a bit thin."

"I get it from baldy here," said Nat, who was getting fed up with the way this was turning out. After all, wasn't she supposed to be a celebrity now?

Dad tried to cover The Bald Spot Which Must Not Be Named with both hands.

"It'll have to do," decided Mrs Hideous.

She reached under the counter and brought out a big plastic tub of what looked like clear jelly.

"This is our own invention. We call it Bio-Organic Gel With A Steady Hold."

"BOGWASH," said Dad.

"Dad!" said Nat, horrified.

"I beg your pardon," said Mrs Hideous.

"The first letters of 'Bio-Organic Gel With A Steady Hold'," explained Dad. "It spells BOGWASH."

"I've ordered five thousand labels from LABELS R US in the town centre now," said Mrs Hideous, who looked like she was regretting letting Dad within a hundred yards of her salon. "DO NOT repeat that. No one's going to want that on their head."

Nathalia stared out of the big glass windows into the street and tried to pretend she wasn't there. *Why did I let Dad talk me into this?* she thought.

As she stared blankly at a queue of people waiting for a bus she saw a very familiar sight. There, fidgeting and talking to himself, was Darius Bagley.

Her first thought was: *Hey, great, Darius, I'll see what he's up to because that's always a laugh.*

Her second thought, about 0.00000001 seconds later was: *DARIUS SHOWED DAD HOW TO MAKE THE WEBSITE AND UPLOAD THAT VIDEO AND RUIN MY LIFE AND SO HE MUST DIE.*

"Just sign the contract, I'll be back in five minutes," yelled Nat, running out of the salon and knocking over a hairdryer.

She hadn't been able to get hold of Darius

for a week now. He didn't have a mobile, or a landline, because the phone company were too scared of his horrible brother, Oswald Bagley, to come round and put one in.

"Stay right there, Bagley, you little worm," shouted Nat, just as the bus pulled up at the stop.

Darius barged to the front of the queue and had almost made it through the door when Nat grabbed his frayed collar and dragged him away. His face was dirty, his hair cropped short and in tufts. He was wearing an old shirt three sizes too big for him and he had a baked bean in his ear.

"Where are you going, looking so smart?" she said. She wasn't being sarcastic – he WAS looking smart. For Darius, that is.

"Let me get on the bus, I'll be late for my job," said Darius, wriggling.

"You've got a lot to answer for," said Nat. "Why did you give Dad that video?"

The last few passengers were getting on as Darius wriggled and squirmed to get away.

"People are watching," said Darius loudly.

"Can't you be normal?"

Everyone in the street stopped and looked at Nat.

"It's her," shouted one man. "It's really her!"

"Can't you be normal?" yelled a woman with a baby buggy. "Ha ha ha!"

"People are watching NOW," shrieked a young shoplifter, who was running past with a toaster under one arm, closely followed by a security guard. The guard slowed down in front of Nat.

"Hey, it's you! Do the dance!" he said.

"Eeek," said Nat, dropping Darius and running back inside the salon. Darius grinned and hopped on the Number 3 bus just as the doors closed.

"Dad, I don't think I want to do this," said Nat, panting, once she was safely back inside the salon.

"Too late!" said Irene Hideous, waving the contract. "It's all signed, sealed and paid for. Now don't worry, this won't hurt a bit."

CHAPTER FIVE

• • • •

WHY HAVE ONE NORMAL HAIRSTYLE WHEN YOU CAN HAVE TEN WILD ONES USING BIO-ORGANIC GEL WITH A STEADY HOLD.

…screamed the poster in the hair salon.

"So, we want pictures of you every day for ten days," explained Mrs Hideous. "Every morning you'll be given a free new hairstyle by our top stylist Suki Glossop. Won't that be exciting?" She was using the sort of pretend-nice voice that mums use when they're trying to get kids to take medicine and the poorly child has already spat it out twice.

"I dunno," said Nat, still shaken from her brush with fame outside.

"Come on – people are going to look at you anyway," said Dad. "At least this way you'll get something out of it."

Yes, and I should be used to being stared at by now, being in your stupid company, Nat thought to herself glumly.

Top stylist Suki Glossop, a young woman with half her head shaved, a collection of piercings and a big tattoo of a dragon up her arm, started fluffing up Nat's hair.

"Get off," said Nat.

"Can you do something with it?" asked Mrs Hideous.

"You're not giving me quality materials to work with," Suki said, sounding very bored.

"Hey," said Nat, "that's me you're talking about. I AM quality materials, thank you very much."

"Just do what you can, OK?" said Mrs

Hideous to Suki Glossop. "You've got Elsie Stain booked in for a shampoo and set at eleven and you know how she gets if we're not ready. Especially if she's started on the sherry early."

"I thought modelling was supposed to be glamorous, Dad," hissed Nat as Suki started preparing her scissors and brushes. "This place is horrible. It smells of burned hair and cats and it's full of mad old people."

"That's why they need you, love," explained Dad. "You're their bit of glamour. You should be flattered."

Nathalia didn't feel very glamorous when her head was shoved in the sink and red-hot water sprayed all over it.

"Ow ow ow!" gasped Nat as her head boiled.

"It needs a hot wash to get the muck out," said Suki, scrubbing shampoo into Nat's tender scalp.

"There's no muck IN," said Nat, offended.

"Sorry, she doesn't wash her hair very much," said Dad. "I'd offer to do it for her, but she says she's too old these days. But this is the result –

manky hair."

"I have NOT got manky hair!" bubbled Nat from the sink, mouth full of shampoo. Her whole head was a big afro of foam. "Shut up, Dad."

Eventually her hair was de-mucked enough for Suki to begin drying, which she insisted on doing with a rough towel, by hand, very hard.

"You're very lucky," said Suki, with a pout. "I wanted to be the hair model, but apparently I'm not as famous as you."

"You're pulling," complained Nat, buried under the scratchy towel. "Ouchy!"

"I can't put you under the dryer – you've got such weak roots they'll just frazzle to a crisp," said Suki.

"Hear that, Dad?" said Nat. "Weak roots. I know where I get those from." Dad put his hand up to his thinning thatch.

"Does she always complain this much?" asked Mrs Hideous, coming over with a tub of the gloopy gel.

"She's not TOO bad," said Dad, who liked

talking about Nat to people when she was sitting right next to him. "Although she moaned and moaned when I wouldn't let her have her ears pierced."

"What's wrong with getting your ears pierced?" said Suki, rubbing Nat's head even harder. *Shuddup*, Dad, thought Nat. *Can't you see this woman's got twelve earrings in each ear??? Not to mention the one in her nose. Or eyebrow. In fact, she's got more piercings than FACE.*

"Nothing WRONG with them," said Dad. "It's just that children look horrible with earrings. Also, it hurts them. Parents who give their kids earrings should be arrested."

"My little Trayvon and D'Shaun have BOTH got earrings," growled Suki. "And they've had them since they were two years old." Nat's head was getting squashed.

"That's nice," said Dad. "Um – is her hair dry now?"

Suki whipped off the towel, grabbed a massive

handful of the gel and slapped it on Nat's head with a splat. Nat could feel it trickling down her neck.

"That's rather a lot," said Mrs Hideous, but then she saw the dark expression on Suki's face and slid off out of the way.

"I think something EXTREME to start," said Suki. "Unless Daddy's little girl can't handle it?"

Nat had had enough of Suki flipping Glossop. Dad might be embarrassing, but this girl was unpleasant and rude. And she was NOT going to let her think she was some silly kid.

Suki began to style. She yanked and pulled and twisted her hair, but Nat wouldn't let on that it hurt. She was a very determined girl and shut her eyes tight and didn't utter a squeak until she heard:

"Finished. Waddya think?"

She opened her eyes and looked in the mirror. She had promised herself that she wouldn't complain NO MATTER HOW HORRIBLE it was.

But it wasn't horrible.

It was wild, it was wacky.

But it was WONDERFUL.

Her new crazy hairstyle was huge and daring and exciting and Nat thought it made her look five years older at least.

It was swept back and up and over and out and high. It made Nat's thin, straight hair look full and curly and spiky and super-glamorous. It was the sort of hairstyle that only miserable-looking models on the front of proper posh magazines have.

Nat posed in front of the mirror, not believing her eyes, ducking down and turning this way and that to see the whole, massive creation.

She LOVED it.

"It's terrible," said Dad.

"It's – flipping – brilliant," said Nat.

"Told you I was good," said Suki, grinning smugly.

Oh my gosh, this is the kind of hairstyle that the cool kids at school will want but their parents won't let them have, thought Nat. Which means that finally, after all this time, I'm actually *one of the cool kids.*

"I don't like it," said Dad.

"Too bad," sniffed Mrs Hideous. "She has to wear it like that *all day*, along with a T-shirt advertising the salon."

She handed Nat a cheap-looking bright red T-shirt with THE FINAL CUT printed on it.

"She can't go out in public like that," said Dad.

"She can and she will. It's in the contract," said Mrs Hideous. "Just above *where you signed.*"

"I can't read that, I left my glasses in the van," admitted Dad.

"Then why did you sign it?" asked Nat.

"Don't interfere," said Dad. "I'm talking business – you won't understand."

"You might have signed me up for anything," wailed Nat. "You could have signed me up for the army, or for scientific experiments. You are rubbish."

"That's not fair," said Dad, feeling a bit

harassed. "You just said you liked the hair."

"Not the point." Nat looked at herself in the mirror. It was true though; she DID like it, so she couldn't be annoyed at Dad for too long.

"Who's doing the photographs?" asked Dad. "Is it one of those paparazzi who take pictures of all the stars?"

"We don't believe in paying photographers," said Mrs Hideous. "It says in the contract you'll take the pictures. It makes it more natural."

It makes it more cheap, you mean, thought Nat, who was feeling less and less like a celebrity by the second.

"I've always fancied myself as a celebrity snapper," said Dad. "I once took a photo of Nat that made it into the local paper. She won a beautiful toddler contest."

"For BOYS," said Nat. "Remember? It was a beautiful boy contest."

"Yeah, but you still won," said Dad. "You got that scooter."

"You said that was from Santa!" said Nat,

remembering the scooter. "You massive cheapskate."

"Now off you go," said Mrs Hideous, who wanted Dad out of her salon as quickly as possible. "Try and take the picture somewhere pretty."

"Round here?" said Dad, laughing. "Not likely – this is the most horrible street in town."

"I live above the salon," said Mrs Hideous, hands on hips.

"And I live next door, above the launderette," said Suki.

"We're leaving now, bye!" said Nat quickly, dragging Dad outside by the hand.

"Be careful with the hair," shouted Suki, just as a massive lorry thundered past. "Don't let it get wet."

"What did she say?" asked Nat as they walked back to the Atomic Dustbin. People were staring at her again, but this time she didn't mind; she knew they were only staring at her AMAZING HAIR. She felt like a film star.

"Dunno, there was too much traffic and I couldn't hear properly. Something about keeping it wet? Probably helps the shine."

"Righty ho," said Nat, skipping along and not paying attention, but checking out her awesome reflection in every shop window. A number 3 bus trundled by.

"Oooh, Dad," she said, reminded of her little monster of a mate. "Can we go and show Darius?"

"No problem. I'll just pop in the mini market for a bottle of water for your hair. I don't want those ladies to think I get EVERYTHING wrong."

CHAPTER SIX

• • • •

F OR ONCE NAT WAS GLAD SHE WAS IN THE HORRIBLE,
huge Atomic Dustbin because at least it had
room for her enormous hair.

"I've got to show Darius," she said, forgetting
momentarily that she was angry with him. "If we
follow the bus route, we might spot him."

"Hmm," said Dad, pulling into traffic.
"Unlikely, and I hadn't planned on spending my
Saturday hunting down Darius Bagley."

"He said something about a job," said Nat,
"but that can't be right."

"Oh, in that case I might know what he's doing," said Dad, in a strained tone of voice Nat recognised as DAD THINKING.

"No one would give Darius a job," said Nat. "They might pay him NOT to work for them."

Dad pulled over in a space that said TAXIS ONLY. He was concentrating. "Lemme think. I was talking to Dolores – that's Miss Hunny to you – the other day," he began.

"I wish you'd stop talking to my form teacher. It's really embarrassing."

"You know we were at college together," said Dad. "When we were young and silly. Oh I could tell you stories…"

"Please, please don't, I'm begging you and I'm not even joking," said Nat, putting her fingers in her ears.

Behind them, an angry taxi driver hooted for Dad to move his van. Dad ignored it. "Anyway, Miss Hunny was saying that Darius got in big trouble last term. Any idea what for?"

Nat had loads.

"Was it putting a baked potato into Mr MacAnuff's exhaust pipe and watching the engine fall out in bits?" said Nat. "Because I don't think anyone knows that was him."

"No, not that," said Dad, who didn't much like Mr MacAnuff the school caretaker so wasn't going to grass Darius up.

"Was it supergluing all the maths books together?"

"No."

"Was it talking so much in double science that Miss Van Der Graaf ran out crying?"

"No."

Nat wracked her brains. There was so much choice. Not ever doing his homework? Singing in French? Writing verses 250 to 253 of his epic poem about poo on the white board? Hiding in the cupboard during history?

"Oh, I know," said Dad, above the sound of angry hooting. "It was not having the school badge on his blazer."

"Not having the *badge*?" said Nat, shocked.

"Dad, that's just stupid. He hasn't got a proper blazer because Oswald keeps selling them. He got an old one from a charity shop, but it was for a different school. It's not his fault, Dad."

"No, but I guess a lot of other stuff IS," said Dad, although Nat could tell he was on Darius's side. "Miss Hunny stood up for him, and she told me she was going to suggest he did something useful for a change. It's supposed to be a sort of punishment, but I thought it sounded like fun."

"What is it?" asked Nat.

"Are you going to shift your ruddy great van from my parking space or are we going to have to take it outside?" said the taxi driver at Dad's window.

"We ARE outside," said Dad.

"Trying to be funny?" said the taxi driver aggressively.

"All the time," said Dad. "It's not easy either."

The angry taxi driver grabbed the door handle and was about to yank it open when he saw Nathalia under her hair.

"Here, it's you!" he shouted, suddenly smiling and showing big gold teeth. "Tell you what – if you say it, I'll let your old dad off without a good beating."

"Can't you be NORMAL, Dad?" shouted Nat. She meant it too.

Eventually, after saying it a few more times, Dad was able to drive off safely.

"Quite useful, you being so famous," said Dad cheerfully. "I bet you're glad Darius gave me that video now."

"Oh, I'm going to show him just how glad I am," said Nat, thinking happy evil thoughts.

It wasn't long before they reached a quieter part of town and soon Dad was slowing down outside a large old house in a street full of large old houses. This one was in the worst state of the lot.

The house was mostly red brick, with large windows and a pointy slate roof. It must have once been a bit grand, but not any longer.

The bricks were stained, the roof crooked and the paintwork on the windows was old and peeling. There was a short drive flanked by two overgrown hedges. Dad turned the wheel and drove in and they bumped over potholes in the drive. Nat could hear a horrible wailing and barking and howling coming from inside the house. She noticed there were FOR SALE signs on the houses either side.

Then she saw a large blue and white sign which read:

PORTER OGDEN'S HOME FOR UNFORTUNATE CREATURES. DONATIONS WELCOME

Underneath someone had handwritten:

I mean donations of money, not more animals. Stop leaving them on the doorstep in cardboard boxes, will you?

"Is Darius living here now?" laughed Nat. "He's an unfortunate animal."

"Very good," said Dad. "But no. This is where he's working at weekends."

"Why?" asked Nat.

"Because Miss Hunny says it'll show Darius what it's like trying to teach him."

"I wish she wasn't your friend," said Nat. "I'd really like to like her." She checked her hairstyle in the rear-view mirror for the tenth time. It was still ace.

"It's gone a bit dry," said Dad, peering at the crazy hairdo. "Shall I sprinkle some water on like we were told?"

"Yeah, whatevs, just hurry up. I want to show Darius before I batter him. He thinks I'm a goody two-shoes. Well a goody two-shoes does not have hair like THIS!"

Dad splashed on a bit of water and Nat hopped down from the van. It was quite a blustery day, but even though litter was being whirled around on the drive, Nat's huge wild hair stayed in place.

"You'd think someone would sweep these streets more often, wouldn't you, Dad?" said Nat, trying to dodge the litter.

"The local paper blames the council," said

Dad. "Your mum blames the government and Bad News Nan blames Europe, television, video games, bad parents, rap videos, footballers, mobile phones, wind turbines, vegetarians, gum chewers and the fact that we can't hang people any more."

"Who do you blame?" asked Nat, batting away an empty crisp packet.

"I just blame people who drop litter," said Dad. "It saves a lot of time."

By now they had reached the stained front door. There were bite and claw marks all over it. The howling and yelping and barking was louder here, and they could also hear frantic scrabbling and crashing as if something horrible was running wild inside.

"I'm sure it's *supposed* to sound like that in there," said Dad, not sounding sure one little bit.

Just as they were about to ring the bell they heard an elderly man's voice: "That's it, Bagley, tempt it back in the cage with that mouse. If that fails, use your hand as live bait."

Nat turned to Dad, hand paused above the doorbell. "Although," she said carefully, "we're back to school next week. I could see him then. PLUS, it might not be Darius in there. He might be talking to a different Bagley."

Something that sounded like a small lion snarled and growled inside.

"Live bait? You can get lost, poo breath," came Darius's voice. "If I put my hand in that cage I won't have a finger left to pick my nose with."

"Simba, in!" shouted the elderly man.

"That doesn't work," said Darius. "You know it doesn't work because you've been shouting that for an hour and Simba is still not in. Do something different to shouting 'Simba, in'."

"Simba?" said Nat.

"Yes, I know, it sounds like a lion's name, but you need to be a zoo to keep a lion," said Dad. He checked the sign. "No, it's not a zoo."

"What's the worst that can happen?" he said, ringing the doorbell.

"Oh," said Dad, looking at Nat. "That's odd."

"What?" snapped Nat, who was already jittery waiting for the door to open.

"That crisp packet has stuck to the back of your hair."

"Get it out then."

"I mean, it's really stuck. Your hair has gone very sticky. It's just a guess, but I think something might have gone a bit wrong."

CHAPTER SEVEN

• • • •

N AT WAS ABOUT TO PANIC OVER HER HAIR WHEN the door opened and an ancient man with a face covered in plasters appeared.

He wore a shredded cardigan, slashed brown trousers, chewed slippers and one lens of his glasses had been smashed.

"Are you from the council?" he said, peering through his broken specs. "Sorry about the noise. And the smell. And all the escaped things. Have you come to put me in prison? It's fine, you know, I don't mind. I could do with a rest from all of this."

Nat wasn't listening; she was trying to pull the crisp packet off her head. This wasn't how she wanted to show off to Darius. As she tugged at the packet, she realised just how glue-like the BOGWASH hair stuff was. Her hand was in danger of getting stuck as well and she yanked it away with difficulty.

"I don't even mind sharing a cell with Sid the Sidcup Strangler," said the old man desperately. "That's nothing to the horrors I've seen in this house. Nothing, I tell you."

"Oi, Buttface, awesome hair," said Darius from the hallway. He was wrestling something fierce in a sack. Nat grew an inch with pride. She stopped trying to unstick the crisp packet.

As long as I don't turn my back on him... she thought. *Which is just as well when it comes to Darius Bagley anyway, to be honest.*

The man at the door – who presumably was

Porter Ogden – eventually let Nat and Dad inside.

The place was chaos, a total mess. Nat had never seen anything like it. Every room in the big, dingy, smelly old house was taken up with cages and tanks and boxes of animals. And not just ANY animals.

There were creatures of all types and all sizes, with only one thing in common: they were all incredibly ugly.

There were three-legged cats and birds with squashed beaks. There were terrible toads, nasty-looking newts and hideous humpbacked snakes. There were dogs with drooling faces so unpleasant, Nat thought they'd have put even Bad News Nan off her Hobnobs.

Even the goldfish were vile enough to give a shark nightmares.

And the animals were EVERYWHERE – some running wild, others pacing or flapping or slithering about in their cages and tanks.

The place ponged.

"I can't open a window since the last great escape," explained Mr Ogden. "I'm used to the smell, but visitors might find it's a bit rich."

Nat's eyes were watering. "Can we go into the garden?" she gasped.

"Good idea," said Mr Ogden. "Bagley, stop playing with Simba and open the back door. I hope no one's scared of emus, wolves, llamas, pigs or howler monkeys?"

Darius shoved the sack in a cage and ran through the filthy, cluttered kitchen to open the back door.

They all tumbled out into the sunlight and the slightly fresher air. The garden was half overgrown like a jungle, half dug up and muddy, and contained various huts and pens.

"It's great, innit?" said Darius, eyes shining.

"Darius, it looks like a First World War battlefield plonked down in the middle of a mad garden centre taken over by zombie animals," said Nat.

"I know – how cool is that?" said Darius. An

astonishingly ugly monkey leapt from a bush on to Darius's shoulder and stuck a banana in his ear.

"I didn't know you had another brother," said Nat.

"Good one. I might have a banana in my ear, but you've got a plastic bottle in your hair," said Darius. Nat realised it was true.

She yanked out the bottle and threw it at Darius's head. He ran off and hid in some bushes. Nat was about to follow him when something from inside the bush howled, so instead she went back to Dad and the elderly man.

"Hope it eats you," she shouted into the bush.

"I take care of all the pets no one wants, not even the rescue homes," Porter Ogden told them. "The ugliest and the naughtiest."

"No wonder Darius likes it here," said Nat. "He'll fit right in."

A llama with a warty face ambled up to Nat and began nibbling the leaves that had got stuck in her hair. "Gerroff!" she said. The llama licked her cheek and she couldn't help giggling.

"It's a nice thing to do," said Dad, who was trying to ignore what a drooling bald poodle was doing up against his leg.

"Tell that to the council," said Mr Ogden and sat down miserably on a rock, which promptly moved: it was a giant one-eyed tortoise with a limp. "Sorry, Desmond," the man said, getting up and taking a crumpled letter out of his back pocket. He showed it to Dad. It read:

ONE-MONTH EVICTION NOTICE.

"What does that mean?" asked Dad. Porter Ogden looked at him as if he was an idiot. "It means the council wants to sell my house and my garden from under me to some developers to build a carpark," he said.

"On the bright side, we could do with some better parking round here," said Dad.

"What'll happen to the animals?" asked Nat, with her arm around the warty llama.

"Dunno," said the old man. Nat thought he looked totally done in. "Darius says I should open the cages and let them sort it out among themselves. See who's left at the end. He says it's nature's way."

"That's horrible," said Nat.

"I'm not going to do that," said Mr Ogden with a smile. Underneath the grime Nat saw he had a kind face. "But I'm the last hope for this lot."

"That's how I feel about Darius," said Nat.

"If it's not rude of me to ask," said Porter Ogden, "why have you got bushes growing in your hair?"

"Oh, what?" asked Nat, reaching up. Instead of hair, all she could touch were leaves and twigs, blown by the brisk wind, and all stuck fast with Bio-Organic Gel With A Steady Hold.

"Just once, Dad, I'd like you to do something for me that doesn't end horribly," Nat wailed. "I look like a tree! I won't be in a fashion magazine, I'll be in a garden centre catalogue."

Dad whipped out his phone and pointed it at her.

"I'll take some photos before it gets any worse," said Dad. "You never know, this might be the next hit hairstyle."

Nat threw her hands up in horror. "You're not taking pictures of me like this!" she yelled. "I'll be an even bigger joke than I am now!"

She was about to throw some llama dung at him when Mr Ogden said, in a fierce whisper that sounded genuinely frightened: "Keep completely still, both of you. Simba is on the loose again."

CHAPTER EIGHT

• • • •

AND THERE, SNARLING BY THE BACK DOOR, STOOD the most horrible, the most ugly, the most downright evil-looking creature Nat had ever seen.

"What is THAT?" croaked Nat.

"We don't really know what she IS, but she's quite grumpy," said Darius, who had appeared like a scruffy ninja next to Nat. He still had the monkey on his shoulder.

The creature was a 'sort of' cat. In the way the Hound of the Baskervilles is a 'sort of' toy poodle.

"Stand completely still," said Mr Ogden.

"One false move and she'll tear your face off."

"Right," said Dad, "what moves are not false? Can I, for instance, leg it back into the house and into the van?"

"That's the *most* false move you can make," said Mr Ogden. "Best not to move at all."

"Until WHEN, exactly?" said Dad. "I have things to do."

"No, you don't, Dad," said Nat. "You never have anything to do."

"Don't move until she sees something other than us," said Mr Ogden. "Like that little bird there, by the pigsty."

On the wooden fence of the sty sat a blue and white bird, preening her pretty feathers. Simba bared her sharp fangs, ready to pounce.

"That poor bird," said Nat. "It doesn't stand a chance."

The cat stalked steadily towards her prey, tail stiff behind her like a javelin. Nat, who hated to see animals suffer and certainly didn't want to see them munched, shouted:

"Fly, little bird, fly!" at the top of her voice.

The bird took off just as Simba leapt. She missed by inches, sharp claws grabbing thin air.

"That'll teach you, bad kitty," scolded Nat.

Simba landed on a patch of mud, looking for the bird. Which flew straight into – Nat's leafy hair. And stuck fast.

"AAAAAGH!" screamed Nat, running around in circles as the bird flapped and struggled and got more and more stuck. "Get it out, get it out!"

"Simba's coming for you," said Mr Ogden. "Run!"

"Dad, this is all your fault!" shrieked Nat as Simba chased her around the garden.

"We don't have much luck with birds," admitted Dad, making a grab for it but missing.

He started to tell Ogden the story about them both getting chased up a tree by a furious goose, then Darius butted in, trying to tell the story of Dad and some very unfortunate French ducks.

"Stop telling bird stories and stop it pecking

my head," shouted Nat, who was being attacked from above and behind. Hot on her heels, Simba hissed and spat at her, leaping to get at the bird.

"DO SOMETHING, Dad!" yelled Nat, disappearing behind a hedge.

"I'll fetch the sack," said Dad, chucking his phone to Darius and springing into action. "What does it like to eat?"

"My face," said Mr Ogden bitterly.

Dad chased after the cat. "Nat, stand still so I can grab it," he said.

"Not likely!" shouted Nat. "It'll have all the skin off the back of my legs."

"That was a close one," said Porter Ogden. "Keep your knees up!"

"This is not what celebrities do on the weekend!" yelled Nat.

The monkey on Darius's shoulder chattered happily at the chaos.

Finally, with Darius and Mr Ogden chasing too, Dad was near enough to risk a leap. Holding the sack in front of him, he launched himself at the horrible beast. Dad landed face-down with a splat in something he hoped was mud but suspected wasn't.

But the sack at least landed squarely on Simba. Dad scooped the creature up just as the bird finally tore free of its sticky nest on Nat's head, taking a large amount of hair with it.

"There you go – all better," said Dad, after he'd locked Simba into a cage. "No harm done!"

He looked at Nat.

"NO – HARM – DONE?" she shouted. "Look at my hair!"

Her entire head was a mass of leaves and twigs and feathers and bird poo and strands of yellow matted animal hair. She looked like a scarecrow whose head had exploded.

"It might need a bit of, um…" began Dad, trying to think of the right words.

"Pruning?" said Darius helpfully, slipping Dad's mobile into his back pocket.

Nat threw something large and sticky at his head.

CHAPTER NINE

. . . .

NAT INSISTED THEY DRIVE BACK TO THE SALON IMMEDIATELY for emergency repairs. She refused to talk to Dad on the way and, as soon as he pulled up, ran into the hairdresser's with an old blanket covering her head.

"You look like an armed robber going into court," said Darius, who tagged along for the ride.

Top stylist Suki Glossop threw up her arms in shock and refused to touch the tangled mass of horror. Manager Irene Hideous ripped up Nat's modelling contract and threatened to sue Dad for making her salon look rubbish.

Nat went straight home and spent the rest of the afternoon locked in the bathroom with six bottles of untangling shampoo. By the time she emerged that night, pink-faced and hungry, her hair and her temper were both pretty much under control.

"I've found a way to make it up to you, love," said Dad as he took a tray of oven chips out.

"I've found my own way, thanks," said Nat. "Staying indoors until everyone forgets about me."

"That'll be ages," said Darius, wandering in eating a pork pie and splattering crumbs everywhere. "Your video's reached one million hits on YouTube today. Course, it got a boost when I linked it to the one of you and Simba."

"Why are you here?" said Nat, wiping spitty pie off her jeans. And then:

"Wait, ME AND SIMBA? Who the flipping heck filmed me and...?" Then she realised.

"You are literally dead, Bagley."

"It's for your own good," said Darius, dodging behind a cupboard. "You only get one chance at being famous and I'm gonna help you STAY famous."

"Come out and be throttled." She grabbed him by the collar and dragged him out.

"Just look at these comments your videos got," croaked Darius. "You'll be pleased, honest."

Nat stopped mid-throttle and had a look. *Flipping heck*, she thought, *Darius is right, most of them are actually nice.* She felt a tiny twinge of guilty pleasure.

Comedy Gold, wrote WheresMeJumper, **put her on TV RIGHT NOW.**

It's better than the rubbish we get on the BBC, wrote JamesBondRunsMyChipShop.

Good but it would be better with vampires in it, said GothGirlUndeadRule

It's the only thing that stops me watching Frozen, wrote LetItGo200

I Dig Mines, wrote I_Dig_Mines, **but I dig the normal girl even more!**

I love the Normal Girl, wrote Silver Surfer Doreen, **she's like my grand daughter in Australia. It's so far away. I'm so sad.**

"Don't read the ones at the bottom," said Darius. Nat couldn't resist a peek.

"Ew," she said, pulling a face.

"Told you," said Darius.

"We've had all these great job offers for you too, so while you were in the shower, Darius and I have been brainstorming," said Dad, pointing to a screen of emails on his laptop. "We've got some great fresh ideas. Darius is very good at blue-sky thinking."

"Stop talking like that," said Nat. "No one knows what that means."

"You need an agent now you're famous," said Darius.

"That's me," said Dad. "And Darius is going to be my assistant."

"I DON'T WANT TO BE FAMOUS," shouted Nat. "Look what happened today. It was a disaster!"

"A disaster today is a chance to learn," said Dad.

"Or maybe it's like a friend you haven't met yet," said Darius.

"Anyway, we've been reading up on the inter cyber-space web on how agents speak and it's something like that," said Dad.

"And I'm not going to be Darius Bagley any more," said Darius Bagley. "It's not a very showbiz name."

"What name do you want, then?" asked Nat.

"Elvis Greed Bugatti," said Darius. "Elvis to you."

"You're mad, both of you," said Nat. "Totally bonkers. And there is ABSOLUTELY NO WAY I am going to let either of you talk me into doing anything more. I've had my taste of fame and I'm not interested. OK?"

Nat had made up her mind. She was

DEFINITELY not going to be famous any more, even though a teeny-tiny, tidgy bit of her was a teeny-tiny tidgy bit pleased with all the attention she was getting. And by the time Dad had fried up something brown in a pan and slopped it over the oven chips, Nat had given herself a proper telling off for liking the attention.

Stop being so vain, she scolded herself. *Before you know it, you'll be ordering fresh flowers and new kittens every day for your bedroom and demanding that the whole street gets painted pink to match your shoes.*

Fame does terrible things to people, she thought.

She was ever so much not interested.

"Just in case I WAS interested – which I'm not – what sort of plans have you been thinking about?" she said.

"The first one is called a voice-over," said Dad. "You wouldn't even have to show your face. Or your hair."

"What's it for?" said Nat, who was not at

all interested.

"WAKE UP!!!!" shouted Elvis Greed Bugatti in her ear.

"Eeek!" said Nat, almost falling off her chair.

Dad waved a leaflet under her nose. "It's a new brand of fizzy drink, called 'Wake Up!!!!'. They're doing a radio advert and they want a fun new voice."

Nat took the leaflet. It was printed in very bright colours.

"I don't like fizzy pop," she said.

"Yeah, but I do," said Darius/Elvis. "And we get loads of bottles for free."

"We?" said Nat.

"We'll get paid too," said Dad.

"We?" said Nat, again.

There was a huge roar outside as Darius's brother Oswald pulled up on his horrid smoky black motorbike. Darius ran to the door.

"I'll get my people to call your people," he said, leaving. Dad gave him the thumbs up.

"Come on," said Dad, "you go into a nice

warm comfy studio next week, read a few lines and go home with pop and pocket money. What's the worst that could happen?"

"If you and Darius Bagley have organised it, the worst that could happen could be really really bad, awful, so I'm absolutely definitely not doing it, OK?" said Nat, her resolve hardening. "And that's final."

It wasn't final at all.

CHAPTER TEN

....

N AT SIGHED AS SHE WALKED TOWARDS THE FAMILIAR big school gates on Monday morning. She felt a bit sick, and not just because Dad had made spam fritters for breakfast.

Just for once I'd like not to be dreading school, she thought. She had no idea what the reaction was going to be to her recent video fame, but she was praying it might have all died down a bit by now. No one seemed to take any notice of her at least. A little butterfly of hope fluttered up in her chest. *Maybe, just maybe, everyone's forgotten...*

But then a couple of annoying Year 7 girls pointed at her and giggled. One did the hoppity little dance of rage that Nat had become famous for. Her fragile butterfly of hope was squished under the heavy bin lorry of reality.

Already? thought Nat. *And I'm not even IN school yet.*

She looked for Darius for a bit of back-up for when she had to face the class, but saw he was already being dragged out of the playground by Miss Austen.

Quick work, Darius, thought Nat. *Impressive...*

Nat dragged her feet as she approached the classroom door. She could hear the laughing of her classmates coming from inside the room. *I'll give you something to laugh about*, she thought miserably. Her hand went slowly to the doorknob. She tried to screw her face into an 'I don't care, la la la' expression and pushed open the door.

"Can't you be NORMAL?" sang her

classmates, and even her form teacher, Miss Hunny, who had joined in.

"You too, Miss?" said Nat, feeling betrayed. Miss Hunny looked a bit sheepish.

"It's all in good humour, Nathalia," she said, smiling, but seeing Nat looking properly sorry for herself, she turned to the class and said, "No more teasing."

"Even if you join in?" asked Marcus Milligan.

"I'm not going to join in," said Miss Hunny, with a tight smile.

Nat scowled and sulkily sat down next to Penny.

It was clear everyone had seen the 'Can't you be normal?' video (as well as the Simba one) and she lost count of the number of times that her classmates whispered the flipping catchphrase at her. The only person who hadn't seen it was Penny, who didn't like the Internet because she believed aliens used it to control people. It was often quite difficult for Nat to resist shouting, "Can't you be normal?" at Penny.

After registration it was double maths because, thought Nat sourly, *It's ALWAYS double maths on Monday morning, it's the law.* On the plus side, Mr Frantz wouldn't have seen the video. He was so old Nat didn't think he even knew what a computer was.

Mr Frantz, who was always sweaty and harassed, got even more stressed and moist as pupil after pupil asked him what the NORMAL answers were. This might have been funny, except Nat knew who the joke was really on.

After first break, which Nat spent hiding in the girls' loo, it was English with Miss Hunny. While everyone was reading some boring Shakespeare that didn't make sense and was about as funny as a plate of school shepherd's pie, Miss Hunny came over and sat down gently next to Nat. Her famous pupil ignored her, pretending to be concentrating on the rubbish play.

"Lots of people think being famous is quite nice," said Miss Hunny.

Nat always found it hard to stay angry with

Miss Hunny because her teacher was actually rather sweet, and was one of the few people who ever stuck up for Darius.

"Lots of people think teachers are quite nice too," said Nat. "Lots of people are wrong."

"Ouch. Point taken. You know, when I was at college with your father—"

"La la la, fingers in ears, not listening."

"Take your fingers out. That's better. As I was saying, we were both in lots of plays together."

"So?"

"Our biggest success was in 'Romeo and Juliet'. We were Romeo and Juliet."

"Miss, I feel sick and I'm not even joking."

"Just listen. It was really interesting because all the boys played the girls' roles and all the girls did the boys' parts."

"Why?"

"It's the sort of thing people do at college to make themselves look clever. It doesn't really matter why."

"So Dad played – *Juliet*?"

"Mmm. He had the legs for it."

"That is so rank."

"Here's the thing. You might think your dad would be embarrassed about it," said Miss Hunny.

"No, Dad's not embarrassed by anything."

"That's because it's much harder to tease someone for doing something if you know they're having a brilliant time doing it," said Miss Hunny.

"I don't understand," said Nat, looking confused.

Miss Hunny underlined a few words in Nat's book.

"I'm going to ask the class what this means in ten minutes," she said. "I want you to answer." She patted Nat on the head and walked to the front of the class. Nat looked at her book, deep in thought.

"'Some are born great, some achieve greatness, and some have greatness thrust upon them,'" read out Miss Hunny, a little later. "What do we think that means? Anyone?"

A few of the swotty pupils put their hands up, but not Nat. She was still desperately trying to work out what the heck her stupid teacher was on about.

"Oh, we always choose you, Sidney," said Miss Hunny, looking at the class's biggest swot. "Let's hear from someone else." A few more pupils raised their hands. Nat was still frowning.

"Anyone else?" Miss Hunny sighed. No more hands. "Very well." She turned to Sidney Slope, whose arm was the straightest.

But then...

"Please, Miss – I know," said Nat, standing up. The class tittered.

"Sit down and be normal," said Becky.

"Simba, no, bad kitty," said Julia Pryde.

"Hilarious," said Nat coldly, in her best Mum Voice. The tittering went quiet.

"It's about getting famous," said Nat, absolutely sure she now understood what Miss

Hunny meant. "You can be born famous like the Queen, you can work really hard to get famous like on *The X Factor*, or you can get accidentally famous."

"Like you!" said Sidney Slope, annoyed that he hadn't been allowed to answer the question.

"No, not like me at all," said Nat with a big grin on her face. "Is that what you really think?"

Her classmates looked puzzled. Miss Hunny tried to hide her smile.

"You don't put hilarious videos of yourself pretending to do silly things online without WANTING to be famous," said Nat, fibbing as hard as she could. She saw everyone's face change and it gave her the confidence to finish with an even bigger whopper.

"Those videos are SO hard to fake, but I'm ever so pleased that you all fell for it. I'm enjoying being a celebrity these days. I mean, who wants to be NORMAL?"

There was a massive pause. Then, right on cue, the bell went and Nat, on a roll, said:

"Must dash. I'm due a call from my agent."

And with that, she left the classroom, grinning from ear to ear.

On her way to the canteen, Nat swung by the Head's office to see if her agent was ever coming back to lessons. But Darius had gone. She was about to head off to lunch when she overheard the Head talking to Miss Hunny in her office.

"Are you SURE this job is working?" said the Head. "I mean, I do like the thought of the Bagley boy getting munched by horrible animals every weekend, but he's still pretty naughty. Do you know he's insisting we call him Elvis Greed Bugatti?"

"Give it time," said Miss Hunny. "I really think this job is giving him the sense of responsibility he needs."

"You'd better be right," said the Head. "Because at the moment, that animal home is the only thing between Darius, or whatever he's currently calling himself, and the exit door."

Nat didn't hear the rest because Miss Austen arrived and gave her a detention for eavesdropping.

"Run along now. And do TRY to be normal," sniggered Miss Austen.

No one teased Nat all through lunch. It was great, and only slightly spoilt by having to explain to a confused Penny Posnitch what was going on.

"So do you really have an agent?" asked Penny.

"Yes, of course," said Nat, with a flick of her hair. "All famous people have to have one."

"I see," said Penny with a sigh, getting up and drifting off.

You can upgrade your phone, why can't you upgrade your friends? thought Nat in exasperation.

And then, as if by magic, that was EXACTLY WHAT HAPPENED.

Because just at that moment, the amazing, beautiful, talented and all-round school superstar

Flora Marling, the most popular girl EVER, sat next to her. ON PURPOSE. And not just because there wasn't anywhere else to sit.

Before she even saw her, Nat smelt her. Flora Marling always smelt of sunlight dancing over fields of flowers. Which was like the opposite of Darius, who smelt of compost.

Flora bent over Nat to say hello and her amazing golden tresses fell lightly on Nat's neck.

"I bet you've never had a bird and a cat fighting in your hair," said Nat as Flora sat down next to her.

Flora frowned and Nat went red. *Why do I say such stupid things?* she thought. *It's Dad's fault – he says stupid things and now he's given me the habit.*

"No, that's never happened," said Flora. "You do have an interesting life."

"I don't want an interesting life," said Nat, "I want a normal one." Aaarrgh! It was out before she could stop it.

"Ha ha, your catchphrase," said Flora, smiling.

"It's ever so funny. Do you like being famous?"

"I'm not famous," stammered Nat.

"My big sister's a model," said Flora, getting more awesome by the second. "She says it's boring."

"Yeah, I was doing some modelling at the weekend, actually," said Nat, trying to look bored. "It *was* boring."

"Yeah," said Flora.

"Yeah, really *really* boring," said Nat. "Nothing happened at all."

"That's so cool," said Flora.

The two girls sat in silence, both looking thoroughly bored.

Just as she was about to leave, Flora said casually "Got anything else lined up?"

"No – oh, actually yeah, a voice-over for a commercial," said Nat, that instant deciding in her head *she was going to do it.*

"So tedious," said Flora.

"I know, but work is work. When you're hot, you're hot."

Shuddup, Nat, you're sounding like an idiot, she screamed inside, but Flora just nodded in agreement.

"Hey, my lame-o parents are going on some kind of cruise for some anniversary or other, whatever. They said I could have some friends over for my birthday. Not a *party*, they made that quite clear." Flora snorted. "But my big sister's throwing me a party anyway in our little pool house."

OMG, thought Nat. *This was the greatest event to hit the school in the history of the world. Every girl would quite literally murder their granny and eat their pet hamster on toast to be invited to Flora Marling's pool party.*

But what was this? Flora was still talking. "If you wanna come, you can. It'll be dull, but you're welcome."

Nat couldn't speak.

"OK, so you're probably busy," said Flora, getting up.

"You're having a secret mega birthday pool

party?" squawked Nat. "And I'm invited?"

"I guess," said Flora.

"OK then," said Nat in a strangulated voice, "that would be flipping awesome – I mean – yeah, I guess, sure, why not? I'll get on to my agent and clear my diary."

Oh, I sound like an absolute spanner, she thought. But Flora smiled.

"Right, see you."

After her heartbeat was roughly back to normal, she ran to find Elvis Greed Bugatti and tell him she'd changed her mind about the voice-over. She was definitely going to do it. If fame had got her an invite to Flora Marling's pool party, then fame was something she wanted more of. *Famous people change their minds all the time*, she reasoned. And besides, Dad was right. What was the worst that could happen?

CHAPTER ELEVEN

. . . .

THE STUDIO WHERE NAT WAS RECORDING HER FIZZY pop voice-over was in a shed on an industrial estate. The shed was a low, steel building with a flat roof sandwiched between a garage and a bicycle repair shop. Nat and Dad stepped over rusty coils of wire and dark puddles to get to the front door.

More glamour, thought Nat sourly, trying to wipe engine oil off her trainers.

Inside, the studio was dim and smelt of car batteries and damp. They were met by a harassed-looking girl doing work experience there who had no idea who Nat was. They waited for half an hour in a draughty room until a red-faced man with a beard and a very loud voice came in.

"GLAD YOU COULD MAKE IT," shouted the man. "I'M MAX, THE SOUND GUY."

"Nice to meet you," said Dad. "My daughter here promises to give one hundred and ten per cent." Dad grinned because he was about to make a bad joke: "And as her agent, I'm taking the ten per cent."

There was a long pause.

"You'll have to speak up, he's almost totally deaf," said the work experience girl.

"I USED TO RECORD HEAVY METAL BANDS," shouted the sound guy.

"If you're deaf, how will you know if I get it right?" asked Nat.

"I'M REALLY GOOD AT LIP-READING," shouted Max. He frowned and shook his head: "CAN YOU HEAR BELLS?" he asked. "OR IS THAT JUST THE RINGING IN MY EARS?"

Nat looked at her dad. "I'm supposed to be FAMOUS. Why is *everything* I do total and utter pants?"

Max handed them a can of WAKE UP!!!! fizzy pop. "THE COMPANY SENT A DOZEN BOXES FOR US ALL. YOU KEEP THEM. I HAD ONE CAN YESTERDAY AND I HAVEN'T BEEN ABLE TO SLEEP SINCE."

Nat pulled a face and put her can down behind a pot plant. Dad immediately opened his and drank it. He shuddered, and then smiled.

"Blimey, there's a kick to that," he said.

Max took them into the small sound booth. There were carpets on the walls and a big round microphone on a stand.

"WHEN YOU SEE THE GREEN LIGHT, I'M RECORDING, SO READ THE SCRIPT," said Max, indicating a green bulb on a long stalk next to the microphone. He handed Nat a piece of paper with the WAKE UP!!!! script on it.

Max went into an adjoining room with a big recording desk in the middle of it. There was a smoked glass screen between him and Nat. He gave her the thumbs up and the green light came on.

Nat was about to start reading when Dad said: "What's her motivation?"

"WHAT?" shouted the deafened Max, turning the light off.

"Motivation. If she's selling this drink, *why* does she like it?" asked Dad. "It'll make her performance better."

"Shut up, Dad," said Nat.

"JUST READ THE SCRIPT, PLEASE. USE THE VOICE YOU DID FOR YOUR VIDEO. GET ON WITH IT BECAUSE I'M DOING A RADIO FOUR COMEDY IN HERE IN TEN MINUTES. WHICH INCIDENTALLY MAKES ME GLAD I'M DEAF."

"Can we just talk it through?" said Dad. "I'm thinking about my client's career. She can't be rubbish."

"Dad…" said Nat.

"RUBBISH IS FINE. IT'S FOR A RUBBISH DRINK. JUST GET A MOVE ON."

"I'm not happy," said Dad. "We can't work like this!"

"Yes, we can, shuddup, I'm starting," said Nat, pushing Dad out of the way and looking at the script. "Put the green light on."

She gave Dad a fierce look as he opened another can of WAKE UP!!!! He was getting as twitchy as Darius.

"Are you sure you should be drinking more of that?" said Nat, but then the green light came on and she had to start reading.

"Hey, kids," she began.

"Don't start with 'Hey, kids'," interrupted Dad, standing in the corner like a naughty schoolboy.

"What's wrong with 'Hey, kids'?" said Nat.

"No one talks like that," said Dad. "I know how children talk. They say, 'What's up, dude?' Or, 'Yolo, bro, how's it hanging? Safe.' Everyone knows that."

"I'm not going to say 'Yolo, bro, how's it hanging, safe', Dad," snapped Nat. "So just stop talking."

She cleared her throat and began again.

"Hey, kids," she said, "it's time to wake up to our new super-fun drink that's fizz-tastic."

"Cut," said twitchy Dad.

"Now what?" said Nat.

"That's not going to wake anyone up," said Dad, glugging down the contents of another can. "I mean, you sound like you've been drinking super-sleepy bedtime hot chocolate, not super-fizzy action pop."

"Will you stop interfering?" asked Nat.

"Just put some LIFE into it," said Dad energetically. "BE the pop."

"How can I BE the pop?" said Nat.

"It's called acting," said Dad, who, let's not forget, had been Juliet in a play at college and now knew everything there was to know about acting.

Nat took a deep breath.

"HEY, KIDS – WAKE UP!!!!" she shouted. "Drink our new fizzy pop. Unless you want a normal life…"

She paused for effect.

"...and who wants to be normal?"

"Cut," shouted Dad again. He was starting to sweat now. "That's your catchphrase. If they want to use your catchphrase they have to pay extra. I told them this. Darius even wrote it into the contract."

"Darius could not have written it into the contract because he can't spell 'extra'," said Nat.

"He can't even spell 'Darius'. He can do sums like a calculator, but he can't write for toffee. And the reason no one knows he can't spell is because none of the teachers at school can read his handwriting. You might as well have got the dog to write it."

"HAVE YOU FINISHED?" asked the sound guy. "ONLY I LEFT MY GLASSES IN THE CAR SO I CAN'T REALLY TELL WHAT'S GOING ON."

"That's it," said Nat, chucking her script on the floor. "We're going home."

She leaned into the microphone and said: "Drink this stuff, don't drink it. I couldn't care less." She looked at Dad, who was now running on the spot.

"Actually, I do care," she said, changing her mind. "You should see what it's done to my stupid dad. A couple of cans and he's ready to run a marathon. This stuff is awful. It's dangerous and frankly I'd ban it right now. Kids, whatever you do, do not drink this."

She yelled straight into the mic:

"I can't make this any clearer. Parents, do not let your kids drink this drink."

"THAT LOOKS GREAT," said Max the deaf sound guy, squinting through the smoked glass screen. "TONS OF ENERGY – I'M SURE THE DRINKS PEOPLE WILL BE PLEASED."

As it turned out, they weren't pleased.

They were over the moon with joy.

Nat yelling, "Parents, do not let your kids drink this," was guaranteed to make every child who heard the advert demand a can of WAKE UP!!!! immediately. Sales went through the roof.

And the full-length version of the advert, including the row with Dad, won the advertising company a bagful of shiny awards. They even got one for 'best script', which was a bit much.

But that was still to come; for now, Dad loaded up the Atomic Dustbin with free crates of the terrible pop.

"I shouldn't have to work under these conditions," said Nat stroppily as she climbed into the front seat. "I'm FAMOUS now, and popular, and everything you get me to do is embarrassing and horrid. It has to stop. You are the worst agent ever. So you're sacked."

Dad didn't answer. His teeth were clenched and his hands shook.

"Pass me another one of those cans, love," he said. "They're very moreish."

Nat refused and demanded he drive to Porter Ogden's ugly pets' home where she could sack Darius too.

"I'm sorry if I've hurt your feelings, but it's not show friends, Dad," she explained, "it's show *business*."

She sat back and smiled to herself, feeling quite pleased with that line.

CHAPTER TWELVE

••••

WHEN THEY PULLED UP OUTSIDE THE PETS' HOME, the front garden was even untidier than usual, strewn with boxes and old furniture, empty animal cages and packing cases.

"Dad," she said, "look at the sign."

Plastered over the name of the home was a big notice which read:

**CLOSING DOWN – BY ORDER
OF THE COUNCIL.
WITH THE HELP OF BLACK TOWER
ESTATES DEVELOPERS**

Helping you to help us to help ourselves.

"There's nothing I can do about it," explained Porter Ogden once they were inside, over cups of tea in chipped mugs. "There's these developers, offering the council lots of money."

"Where do you want the revolting rats?" asked Darius as he emerged from behind some crates at the back of the cramped kitchen.

"Anywhere," said Mr Ogden. "Just as long as Simba doesn't get a sniff of them. Now come and have a cuppa."

"Don't use the milk from the blue jug," said Darius, clanging about. "It's been out of the fridge for a fortnight."

Mr Ogden quickly hid the blue milk jug behind the biscuit tin and Nat decided she wasn't very thirsty after all.

Dad drank his tea in one gulp. He pulled a face. "That pop leaves a nasty taste in your mouth," he said. Nat decided not to tell him about the milk.

"These developers want to build a block of flats and a car park on top of my house," said Mr Ogden, eyes filling up with tears.

"That's a good idea," said Dad. "The parking's terrible round here." Nat kicked him.

"And now they say I've only got a couple of weeks to get out before the bulldozers turn up and flatten everything."

"That's terrible," said Nat. "Where will you live?"

"Oh, I can have one of the new flats, but it's tiny. I don't care about me, but there's only room for half a dozen three-legged mice."

"Even King Kong's got to go," said Darius, appearing with the scruffy monkey on his shoulder. The monkey combed through Darius's short tufty hair and nibbled something tasty.

"Is there nothing you can do?" asked Dad.

"Not unless you want to take hundreds of unwanted, horrible, ugly, badly behaved monsters home with you?" said Mr Ogden hopefully.

"I will," said Darius.

"Not really," said Dad. "Can't you pay the council more money than the developers?"

"That's a great idea," said Mr Ogden. "I hadn't thought of that. I completely forgot about the million quid I've got stuffed in an empty tin of spam."

"I'm just thinking out loud," said Dad helpfully.

"Well don't," said Nat. "Why don't we all think in silence? Especially you, Dad."

And so they did. Nat didn't need to ask what would happen to all the animals. This home was the end of the line. NO ONE else was mad enough to take them in.

And then she had another horrible thought.

She remembered what the Head had said about Darius – that this job was the only thing keeping him from being thrown out of school. She thought about trying to make him behave and then realised it would be easier to raise one million quid.

"We need a celebrity campaign," said Dad, breaking the silence.

"What's that?" asked Mr Ogden, who was

pretty unsure about Dad's ideas.

"We just need to find a celebrity to get behind the home, and do a campaign to raise money to save it. If enough people want it kept open, the council can't bulldoze you."

"Two problems," said Mr Ogden. "First, no one round here wants this home kept open. Not after the last mass break-out. In fact, when the council stuck that closure sign up outside, the neighbours organised a street party to celebrate."

"Oh, our old neighbours did that when WE moved," said Dad. "It was just their way of saying they'd miss us."

Mr Ogden gave Nat a quizzical look. "Yes," she said. "He is always like this."

"What was the second problem?" said Darius.

"I don't know any famous people."

There was a long pause. All that could be heard was the sound of Simba chewing through iron bars somewhere.

"Well, do you know anyone famous?" asked the old man.

Dad and Darius both looked at Nat. If the home closed, the animals AND Darius would be chucked on the scrapheap, Nat thought.

And then another thought formed. A little evil thought, about being famous and popular and Flora Marling's birthday party.

"OK," said Evil Nat, "you're both un-sacked as my agents and I'll do everything I can to get as famous as possible," adding quickly, "to save the ugly pets, of course."

CHAPTER THIRTEEN

• • • •

Darius stayed over at Nat's house that night, plotting with Dad. Luckily for them, Mum wasn't around to help/tell them off for stupidity, because she had been called away on urgent business. Nat was never quite sure what it was Mum did for a living exactly, but she absolutely knew it was more sensible than whatever Dad and Darius were up to.

She could hear them well into the night, drinking cans of WAKE UP!!!! pop and coming up with ever more nutty ideas on how to make her more famous and save the horrible pets.

Well, as long as it meant she got invited to Flora Marling's mega secret birthday pool party, she didn't really care. She fell asleep that night smiling to herself, thinking about what dress she might wear to the party of the century.

Next morning, Dad drove Nat and Darius to school. He was wearing a suit, which puzzled Nat. She didn't even know he HAD a suit. She wondered if it was actually his suit, because it was about three sizes too small for him. His arms stuck out way past the sleeves and she could see over the tops of his socks.

Dad saw her looking at him. "This suit was a bargain," he said as they drove noisily along in the Atomic Dustbin, all the boxes of WAKE UP!!!! pop clanking and clanging about in the back.

"I ordered it online. I got it made in Bulgaria specially."

"What, by a blind person?" said Nat.

"I might have made a small mistake with my measurements. Stupid inches and centimetres."

"Why are you wearing a suit anyway?"

asked Nat.

"Probably in trouble with the police," said Darius, swigging from a can of bright orange pop. His eyes opened wide. "This stuff is AWESOME," he said.

"Have either of you actually been to bed?" said Nat.

"I'm not in trouble with the police, thank you," said Dad.

"It wouldn't be the first time," said Nat.

"Not fair," said Dad, laughing. "I've only been arrested once and that was on that barge holiday in France. And ANYONE can sink a couple of priceless antique vintage French sailing barges."

"Why ARE you wearing a suit then?" asked Nat. "Don't tell me you've got a job?"

"Back after the adverts," said the witless radio DJ, who was called Cabbage.

"Woof," went the dog, who hadn't said much up until then.

"You sure I can have all these cans?" said Darius.

"Yes, Darius, whatever, do what you want with them," snapped Nat.

"I've got a meeting at the park actually," said Dad. "About YOU."

Nat wanted to ask more, but Dad suddenly turned the radio up.

"It's our advert!" he said. "Listen."

Nat listened in horror as her argument with Dad was broadcast to kids all over the country on their way to school. Finally, it ended with radio Nat yelling: "Do not let your kids drink this!"

The real Nat put her head in her hands.

"You know what this means?" asked Darius.

"I've been humiliated again?" said Nat.

"Oh yeah that. But more importantly, I can sell these at school. Everyone's gonna want a can."

Just then a news item came on the radio saying that due to recent complaints from parents about the terrible effects of a new fizzy pop drink called WAKE UP!!!!, all sales of it were now banned.

"Even better!" said Darius.

"Why? Because they'll stop playing the stupid advert now?"

"Nah," said Darius, with an evil grin, "it means the price of WAKE UP!!!! has now doubled!"

"Why are you helping Darius sell banned pop?" asked Nat as Dad backed the Atomic Dustbin into the school's entrance.

"He said he'd give the profits to the save the ugly pets' fighting fund," explained Dad, watching as Darius took out the crates of banned pop and began hiding them behind the bins.

"MOST of the profits," corrected Darius.

Nat knew the real reason Dad was helping was that Dad HATED rules. Dad never wanted to do anything wrong, right up until the moment someone told him he *couldn't* do it.

Darius was a bit different; he just did what he wanted.

Both of these things made Nat feel stressed. She liked rules, on the whole. They made life simpler. She reckoned she only spent so much time with Dad and Darius to keep them out of trouble. Which she didn't seem to be doing a very good job of so far that day.

In fact, it turned out to be one of those rare days where Darius wasn't sent out of a class once. Instead of his usual hyperactive self, he was strangely quiet. He still didn't do any work, of course, but teachers were so relieved that he hadn't locked anyone in a cupboard or superglued himself upside down off a door or written any more of his disgusting epic poo poem 'Diarrhoea' (now at verse 367) that he got two gold stars and a bar of Fruit and Nut as a reward.

He wasn't even insisting on being called Elvis Greed Bugatti any more. Darius was being… good.

In the playground, Nat overheard Miss Hunny tell the Head that it was all due to her getting him a job at the pets' home. Then Miss Austen slid up with a nasty grin on her face.

"Shame it's being closed down then, isn't it?"

she said, in a voice that made it obvious that she didn't think it was a shame at all, before giving Nat another detention for eavesdropping.

Nat knew the truth about Darius's behaviour: Darius was being good because Darius was Plotting. All day he was scribbling notes and drawing diagrams in a tatty old notebook. She knew it must be important because Darius didn't have many notebooks; his horrible brother, Oswald, ripped them up for a laugh.

She kept pretending she wasn't interested in his plotting all day, right up until home time when her curiosity got the better of her.

"What are you up to?" she said by the school gates. "And why haven't you sold any pop? Have you finally realised it's a bad thing to do?"

"It's called a business plan," said Darius. "You wouldn't understand because you didn't do the online course like me and your dad last night."

He yawned. "Sleep is for wimps," he said, glugging a can of banned pop. "See you in the morning. Get here early."

She didn't get much sense out of Dad that night either, partly because he hadn't slept for a couple of days, but also because Mum was home so they all went for a Chinese and Dad said not to bother Mum with *things they'd been up to recently* as Mum always called it.

This was due to the fact that *things they'd been up to recently* usually made Mum cross.

The next morning – early – Nat tracked Darius down to a hiding place behind the bins, where he'd stashed the pop. He handed Nat half a dozen.

"First, we salt the mine to generate a non-calm market," said Darius.

"What?" said Nat.

"I can't say it any clearer."

"Yes, you can, you big chimp. You can say it loads clearer."

"We're giving twelve cans away for free."

"That's a stupid idea."

Darius ignored her. "But we only give them away free to taste-makers."

"You're doing it again," growled Nat. "Do you want a Chinese burn?"

"We give them to the most popular kids in school. Then, when everyone else sees them drinking WAKE UP!!!!, they'll want a can too. But this time, they'll have to pay."

Nat thought for a moment. "Actually that's quite clever," she admitted. Darius started to shove cans in her schoolbag.

"Oi, I'M not doing it," she said. "I'll get into trouble."

"The faster we sell these, the quicker they'll be gone and the less chance there is of getting caught. You don't want to be caught, do you?"

"Of course not."

"Get a move on then."

"I'm not sure about this," she said, loading up her bag.

"If you keep being negative I'll have no choice but to rationalise my workforce," said Darius.

"Is that bad?" said Nat.

"It is for you – you'll be de-hired," said Darius.

"What?" said Nat.

"Sacked."

"You can't sack me. You're my agent. I sack YOU," said Nat crossly. "Aren't you supposed to be making me famous?"

"Later. Just hand out those cans."

Nat was way too shy to talk to six really popular kids, so she just gave them all to Flora Marling.

"Is that the banned pop?" asked Flora.

Nat went red. "Yeah. Oh, I'm sorry, don't think I'm a bad person," she stammered. "I'm only doing it for a good cause. There's this pets' home and—"

"I don't think you're a bad person. I think you get cooler by the day," said Flora, hiding the cans in her bag. "Thanks."

Nat spent the rest of the day floating on Flora Marling-scented air. *Doing good is really great for your image*, she thought.

CHAPTER FOURTEEN

••••

NAT HAD TO ADMIT DARIUS'S EVIL POP SCHEME worked brilliantly. Over the next week the cans of dodgy drink proved irresistible to every kid at school. Demand for the fizzy menace skyrocketed, as did the price.

Nat was pleased that they were building up a good fighting fund for the pets' home, but a bit alarmed to learn that everyone thought SHE was the brains behind the pop scheme, not Dopey Darius.

"I just did the advert," she would say about a hundred times a day, when someone would ask her for a can, but everyone thought she was joking. Even worse, because it was banned, kids gave the pop a secret code word. They would ask for a can of NORMAL pop, and then wink at her.

"I don't know what's worse," she laughed to Penny one lunch break. "Being famous for doing a silly video, or being famous for flogging dodgy pop."

"Mmm," said Penny, who seemed a bit distracted. *She was looking like that a lot these days*, thought Nat.

"I mean, I don't feel too bad about selling the pop – I'm just providing a service."

"Hmm," said Penny, toying with a chip.

"It's like being famous," said Nat.

"Is it?" said Penny, staring off into space.

"Famous people are providing a service too. People need to look at them. I mean, if no one wants you to be famous, you won't be famous, stands to reason."

"I think I'm getting a stomach ache," said Penny.

"Is it the pizza?" asked Nat.

"No," said Penny, getting up to leave just as Julia Pryde and Trudi Button plonked themselves down by Nat, giggling.

"Where are you going?" said Nat. But then she forgot all about Penny as Julia and Trudi started talking excitedly about what they were going to wear to the social event of the century: Flora Marling's mega secret birthday pool party sleepover.

As the week went on, Nat watched as Darius charged more and more money for each can. His masterstroke was starting a rumour that the last of the cans were almost gone. He was immediately mobbed in the playground by a gang of twitchy kids all offering him more pocket money.

"But we've got lots of boxes of pop left," said Nat as they walked to double geography, looking at Darius's bulging, cash-filled pockets.

"Don't tell anyone that," said Darius. "Have you seen the price I can get these days?" He patted his pockets and grinned. "Supply and demand. They're my two new favourite words."

Nat had a sudden horrible vision of an adult Darius in a business suit sitting on top of a vast evil business empire, finally able to build the underground lair of doom he'd always wanted. The world was NOT SAFE.

"Maybe you should stop now," she said.

"I'm only doing it for the little ugly animals," said Darius.

Nat gave him a hard look. "Are you sure?" she asked. "Only, you seem to be wearing new trainers."

"I have expenses," Darius said, looking shifty. "Anyway, I have to look smart so people trust me," he continued, hurrying to class.

But soon children who'd been drinking the pop began acting very oddly. Teachers were baffled. Lessons were being disrupted by kids shouting and running around and fighting and singing.

"Zis is ein classroom, not ein stadium,"

shouted a harassed Mr Frantz, the tiny old maths teacher one afternoon during a particularly manic lesson.

"Vy are you all behaving like ze football hooligans?"

He would have said more, but a few of the bigger boys had picked him up and were running around the class with him on their shoulders like he'd won the World Cup, chanting:

"He does sums when he wants, he does sums when he wants, ohh, Mister Fra-antz, he does sums when he wants."

"I'm zo glad you like my lesson," said Mr Frantz, confused. "Please put me down und ve can get on wiz fractions."

Soon even the children who hadn't managed to get their hands on WAKE UP!!!! were getting caught up in the mad mood and joining in the school's mayhem. Worse, the naughty kids who normally played truant decided that school finally seemed like a fun place to be and stopped hanging about in the shopping centre. The classrooms had never been so full.

One day it took two hours to get everyone in from lunch break, and that didn't include Benny Prefab from 7C who was doing press-ups in the flowerbeds until home time. He was last seen being carted off under Mr KitKat's arm shouting: "I'm going for two thousand, don't stop me!"

Every day it got worse. The noise became terrible. Classrooms were in uproar. Books and pens and paper and bags and blazers and the less heavy teachers were chucked around willy-nilly.

No work was done at all. Classes and corridors were a blur of running, giggling, jumping children who couldn't sit still for more than a minute, along with the less brave teachers who didn't fancy being passed about the place like a beachball.

The science labs were out of bounds on safety grounds following a small explosion and Mr MacAnuff the grumpy caretaker was in favour of calling out the army.

Nat saw him as he cornered the Head in a corridor at break. "Have you seen what the little devils in Year 10 have done behind my shed?" he wailed.

"It's very good," said the Head. "I'm assuming it's for a project on World War One? Some kind of trench warfare reconstruction?"

"No, it was my rose garden."

"Well, I can't help that," the Head snapped as she watched a shrieking first year cartwheel into the art room. "I'm very busy because I've got a lot of job application forms to fill in."

She hurried off and Nat scarpered before Mr MacAnuff made her plant some more flowers. She went to look for Darius, and found him in the boiler room stuffing money into a tin box. A snivelling boy was pulling at his sleeve, and Nat heard him offer Darius the whole of his next-year's pocket money for another can of WAKE UP!!!!

"I'll think about it," said Darius.

"DARIUS BAGLEY, STOP THIS RIGHT NOW," yelled Nat. She wasn't kidding.

Darius dropped the tin box and looked

incredibly guilty for a second. Then he recovered himself.

"Get lost," he told the boy. "And remember what I said about saving the ugly pets."

"You didn't say anything about saving ugly pets," said the boy and Darius chucked an empty can of pop at his head. The boy ran off.

"Darius, I think you've actually broken the school," said Nat. "Which I have to admit is quite funny. But lately I've been starting to enjoy school for the first time ever and you are not going to spoil it for me."

There was an echo in the boiler room. Nat's last word bounced around the walls:

Me *me me meeee*...

"Now, how much money have you made?" asked Nat.

Darius shoved the cash box roughly at Nat. "Loads," he said, spitting on the floor and rubbing his scruffy hair.

"Darius, there's only £2.50 in here," said Nat.

"Oh," said Darius, standing on one leg and

trying to hide his new trainers.

"That's it: stop selling the stupid drinks," said Nat.

"But I'm popular now," he said with a big sigh. "Everyone wants to talk to me."

Not for the first time Nat went straight from wanting to strangle Darius to wanting to hug him.

"You silly boy," she said gently. "You're still not popular. It's the stupid pop that everyone wants, not you. Everything will go back to how it was before, when you stop selling it."

"Promise? You're not just saying that to cheer me up?"

"I promise. Everyone still thinks you're horrible. And they always will."

"Thanks," said Darius as they walked out of the boiler room together.

"Unlike you," said Darius. "You really *are* popular these days."

Nat was shocked. She didn't *really* think she was popular. She still felt she only had one proper friend – Penny – aside from Darius, who didn't count. *But then*, she thought, *I AM going to Flora Marling's mega secret birthday pool party... And Julia and Trudi DID sit at my table at lunch today...*

Nat felt a warm glow inside as she realised the truth: she was actually becoming popular.

"AND you're famous," Darius continued, "and with all the things me and your dad have lined up next week, you're gonna be really REALLY famous. You'll be up in lights."

"My name's gonna be up in lights," corrected Nat. "That's the expression."

"Whatever," said Darius. "Anyway, then you'll be even more popular."

"Well, whatever it takes to save those ugly pets!" said Good Nat with a virtuous smile, while inside Evil Popular Nat was rubbing her hands together gleefully.

CHAPTER FIFTEEN

• • • •

66 I'VE DECIDED I'M GOING TO DO ALL THE STUPID and rubbish things you've organised for me, Dad," said Nat on Saturday morning as she ate her greasy late breakfast in front of the telly.

"That's good of you," said Dad.

"I know," she said, turning over to a cookery programme in the hope it might give Dad some ideas and stop him frying pork pie slices for breakfast. "I just want to do anything I can to save the horrible pets and the horrible Darius."

"That's my girl," said Dad, with a smile.

"So then," she continued, "I might as well get as famous as possible, as quickly as possible. And then I can get it over with as fast as possible. Now, what do I have to do?"

This is great, she said to herself, looking at the list of events Dad had lined up for her. *And it's got absolutely nothing to do with wanting to be popular*, she massively fibbed to herself.

What made it sweeter still was that she didn't even have to use her real, stupid, mega-embarrassing name. No, as far as most people knew she was Nat the Normal Girl.

It's just like being called Dinky Blue, Girl Guru, she thought, remembering her fave online vlogger. *Her real name is probably something just as silly as mine. She's probably Mary Christmas, or even Barbara Blacksheep.*

Well, that's something else we share, thought Nat. *Along with fame and popularity.*

The following week was the busiest Nat had ever known.

Dad had made some badges with the letters SOUPH on, for her to hand out when she was doing her celebrity events. SOUPH stood for Save Our Ugly Pets Home.

"Souf?" asked Nat on Monday morning, studying one of the badges.

"Soup," said Dad, putting his coat on. "The H is silent."

Nat giggled. "You are rubbish," she said. "Is this the best you could come up with?"

"Yes," admitted Dad, "and I was up all night too. Now stop criticising and just make sure everyone you meet gets one."

On Monday night she opened the new video arcade in town. They had installed a dance machine and wanted her to do her dance on it. She had to admit it was a BIT embarrassing at first, but she was given a stack of free arcade tickets, which she handed out to her new friends at school the next day.

Penny, however, refused to take one. "I'm not

allowed in the arcade," she said as they ate lunch.

"So?" said Nat. "These tickets are like gold dust! Give them to people you like. Or –" she lowered her voice – "and this is the best bit, give them to people who you want to like YOU." Nat waved at a group of girls, who waved back.

"I don't need to buy my friends," said Penny sniffily, walking off. "And you shouldn't either."

"I'm not buying friends!" said Nat, annoyed, but she soon forgot to be annoyed when Julia and Trudi came and sat down with her. *Who needs you anyway, Penny*, thought Nat to herself.

On Tuesday night Nat had her picture taken outside the town theatre, to help advertise their new play. She was going to be on their posters with:

"You'd be hopping mad to miss it!" written just below her picture.

The director, Derek Plungepool, who was wearing a white suit with a bright purple cravat, said she was "just divine" and gave her a row of tickets for the opening night.

This is easy, thought Nat, wondering which of her new friends deserved a ticket. In return she almost forgot to give Derek a handful of SOUPH badges, which he promised to hand out to the cast.

"You are just *gorgeous*, doing all this charity work," he gushed.

"Oh stop," said Nat, smiling for the camera, "it's not me who deserves the applause, it's those little ugly forgotten-about pets."

She had promised to help Darius at the ugly pets' home on Wednesday night. Simba's cage needed cleaning and this was definitely a two-person job.

"Sorry, Little D," she said as they were leaving school.

"Little D? Who's that, Buttface?" said Darius, stunned.

"I'm just TOO shattered to come," Nat replied. "Besides, my nails are totally ruined and I'm going to look *horrible* for my personal appearances if I don't fix them."

"You always look horrible," said Darius.

"I'm doing this for *you*," hissed Nat, running off to join Julia Pryde and some of the other popular girls, who were hanging about at the school gates.

On Thursday evening Nat was due to judge a talent competition at the local old people's home.

"Tonight is a double win," Nat told Penny, who seemed to be barely listening. "They're paying me fifty quid AND my nan's given me a tenner to make sure Edna Pudding loses."

"That is so wrong on so many levels," said Penny.

"I know, I could have got her up to twenty," said Nat. "She hates Edna Pudding."

At lunch Darius gave her a letter that Porter Ogden had received from the developers, Black Tower Estates. Darius was a total maths genius, but he wasn't too hot at reading, so he thrust it under Nat's nose.

"Porter Ogden couldn't read it cos Simba ate his glasses," said Darius, who was covered in big red scratches. "How are your nails, by the way?"

"Fine," said Nat, snatching the letter. "Oooh this is bad, very bad," she said, reading it. "It says that the developers went to see the council, who agree he's standing in the way of progress and fairness and decent behaviour, so in fourteen days' time they're sending in the bulldozers."

"How's the campaign going?" said Darius. "Cos time's running out."

"What's that supposed to mean?" asked Nat defensively. "I'm working my fingers to the bone for you. I hope you appreciate it!"

"You what?" said Darius.

"Forget it, she's been like this for ages," said Penny, sitting down next to them. "Fame's gone to her head."

"That is SO not true and anyway, I'm far too busy to talk right now," said Nat, getting up from the table. "I need to sort out what I'm wearing tonight. The local paper's sending a photographer." And with that she got up and left.

That evening, Bad News Nan invited herself to the old folk's home with Nathalia. Nat didn't really want her to come, because she knew Nan didn't approve of her new-found fame. Or any fame for that matter. Bad News Nan had always said fame was just another word for *showing off,* which was A BIG CRIME in Bad News Nan's world, along with *making a fuss* and *getting above yourself.*

So Nat was a bit puzzled as to why Nan was so keen to introduce herself to everyone at the High Hopes Retirement Villa as "the grandmother of the Normal Girl". Nan had even put her best teeth in. AND she was wearing her big black floppy hat that she usually only wore for special occasions like funerals.

"It used to be my wedding hat," Nan explained as they sat in the big living room and waited for the talent show to begin, "but at my age I see more people buried than wedded, so I had it painted black."

Bad News Nan looked around at the doddery old folks sitting in big squishy armchairs. The room was painted a pale brown, like a gravy stain. It smelt of cabbage and boiled fish. Nan sniffed the air hungrily.

"They have it ever so good in here," said Bad News Nan, rather too loudly for Nat's liking. "Watching telly all day, waited on hand and foot, ooh it sounds lovely. I don't know what they've done to deserve this treatment. Luxury, I call it. Oh, don't fuss, they can't hear me," she said as Nathalia tried to shush her. "They're either deaf or they think it's the radio."

Nan swiped a bowl of custard off one of the helpers, who was clearing leftovers. "And have you tasted this custard?" she said. "They put it through a *blender*. Now that's what I call smooth. Your father never does that for me. No, he doesn't care WHAT lumps I get stuck under my top plate."

The lady who ran the home brought Nat a cup of tea and some dusty ginger cake and thanked her for being a judge.

"We've told everyone you're off the telly," she said quietly, "which is a teeny fib, but it makes them feel you're a bit more special."

"Is there no more ginger cake?" said Bad News Nan. "It'll help soak up this custard. Runny, I call it."

"Is she doing the bingo?" asked Gladys Dogweed, suddenly looming over and peering at Nat, who squeaked in alarm.

"No, she's NOT doing the bingo," snapped Bad News Nan. "This is Nathalia the Normal Girl and she's a star. She'll be selling autographs later."

"Selling?" giggled Nat when Gladys had gone.

"It's costing me ten pounds to make sure that Edna Pudding comes last. I want to get some money back," said Bad News Nan, adjusting her hat. It was so big that no one sitting behind her could see the stage.

"Why do you hate Edna Pudding so much?" asked Nat.

"Don't talk so soft – I don't hate her, she's my best friend," said Nan. "But she's always liked showing off and I don't want her getting above herself. It's not good for her."

She waved at the first talent show hopeful like the Queen.

"You may proceed," said Bad News Nan.

Nat spent the next two awful hours being force-fed horrible ginger cake and enduring pensioner piano-playing, tap-dancing and poetry reading, the highlight of which was Betty Bullwhip's ode to her dead cat:

"Kitty loved her biscuits and milk
  Kitty wandered far
  Kitty's fur was satin and silk
  Until she got hit by that car."

Nat stuffed a huge piece of ginger cake into her mouth to stop herself from hooting with laughter.

She wiped a silent tear from her eye and Mavis Stench came over and put an arm around her.

"Don't cry, dearie," she said. "I'll tell you a secret. It was her husband driving the car. I bet she doesn't mention that."

Nat felt a tiny bit bad at placing Edna Pudding and her accordion last, behind even the terrible dead cat poem, *But a deal's a deal*, she thought, patting Nan's tenner in her back pocket.

At the end of the night, as Nat was putting her coat on to leave, she heard Bad News Nan comforting an upset Edna. "Well, I thought you were very good," said Bad News Nan. "Young people these days don't recognise real talent. Anyway, must dash, it's my knees, all that sitting." She sucked ginger cake off her teeth. "I expect I'll see you at Doris Robinson's funeral."

"Hey, you, I'm still alive!" said a very elderly old lady, shaking her stick.

Bad News Nan ignored her. "Have you got a black hat?" she asked Edna, and they cackled happily together.

CHAPTER SIXTEEN

NAT'S WEEK OF ACTIVITY CONTINUED ON Friday night with the opening of a brand-new bowling alley and ice-cream café at the retail park nearby. It was to be a grand, celebrity-studded affair. Dane Smarm from TV's popular regional daytime quiz show *You're Useless, Get Lost* was coming. So was reality star Ellie Stupid, who had become famous appearing in *The Stupids from Stupid Street.*

But more importantly, also on the guest list was:

NAT THE NORMAL GIRL!

Plus Dad *and two other guests of her choice…*

On Friday morning at school, Nat held the invite with trembling hands, her breakfast toast totally forgotten.

"Why didn't you give me this before, Dad?" she said. "This is like the greatest thing to happen to me, ever."

"Don't be so sarky, I know it's only a bowling alley," said Dad.

"I'm being serious," she said. "Honestly."

"Well, I only got the email from the bowling alley people late last night, while you were at the old folks' home. You were ever so tired when you got back. Besides, you don't like bowling. I wasn't sure you'd want to go."

"I can take two guests," squealed Nat. "Two friends who can see me with other celebrities."

"Yeah, I know it's a bit embarrassing," said Dad. "But you can give out flyers about the ugly pets' home."

"Yeah, course, animals, whatevs," said Nat. "But more importantly, I get to invite two guests to see me with other celebrities."

"You said that already," said Dad. "I suppose you'll take Darius and Penny."

"I do WANT to take them," said Nat slowly, "but Penny's being mean to me and Darius doesn't fit my image."

"Image?" said a very familiar voice in the doorway. "Have I been away long enough for you to have an *image*?"

Mum was laughing in the kind of way that showed she wasn't finding it one hundred per cent funny, but Nat didn't notice; she was just thrilled to see her.

Mum drove her to school in her fast little red car and Nat tried to explain what she had meant. Darius always said Nat's mum was a spy, and though Nat always laughed at him, she knew Mum was very good at getting information out of her, so she chose her words very carefully.

"What I *meant* to say," said Nat as Mum went through a red light, "was that Darius loose in a bowling alley might get the ugly pets' home the wrong sort of publicity."

"Hmmm," said Mum. "Are you sure?"

"We want people to be on our side," said Nat, "and not many people want to be on the same side as Darius."

"I see what you're saying," admitted Mum, "but why do you think Penny is being mean to you?"

"I think she's one of those girls who wants the spotlight on her all the time," fibbed Nat, hoping Mum didn't have some kind of secret agent lie detector in her handbag, as it would DEFINITELY have gone off. Penny didn't even like being filmed doing a dance in Nat's back garden, let alone being 'in the spotlight'.

"Well, I guess it's up to you," said Mum, screeching up at the school gates. "Invite who you like."

So Nat did. She invited Julia Pryde, who shrieked and said Nat was, "TOTES AMAZE!".

Then Nat took a deep breath and walked over to Flora Marling, just before they went into double science.

"Thanks so much," said Flora. "Aren't you taking Darius and Penny with you?"

"They can't make it," fibbed Nat, feeling terrible.

"Cool," said Flora.

"Great," said Nat, feeling FLIPPING BRILLIANT.

"I heard that," said Darius, sitting down next to Nat.

Nat jumped. "I thought you were in the Room Of Doom," she said.

The Room of Doom was actually called the Chill-out Centre. It had little individual cubicles. Naughty kids had to sit quietly and draw pictures and listen to soothing music until they promised to behave. It was run by a mild-mannered teacher called Mr Hibbert.

"Mr Hibbert is off with stress," said Darius, eyeing up the cupboard full of chemicals. "He threw the CD player out of the window and said he couldn't listen to the soothing music any more, it was driving him round the bend."

There must be better schools than this, thought Nat. *Maybe if I get rich…*

Darius stuck a compass into a gas tap. "Anyway, I think it's a good plan of yours to invite Marling – she's bound to get photographed."

"I'M the celebrity being photographed," said Nat huffily. "Not her!"

"Yeah, but you look like a squashed goblin next to her," said Darius. "Get real. Just make sure she's wearing a SOUPH badge."

At the bowling alley that night, Nat didn't even care that Darius was right and the local photographer spent all his time taking pictures of Flora.

She didn't care that Dane Smarm was rude to her and Ellie Stupid didn't show up because she got lost on the way.

She didn't care that she had forgotten all the SOUPH badges.

She didn't care that she was made to do her stupid dance yet again, or that it was so crowded that she kept getting trodden on, or that they weren't even given a single free ice cream.

She didn't care because, just as they were leaving, Flora Marling said to her:

"That was fun. Don't forget, it's my secret birthday pool party sleepover a week on Saturday. All my friends will be there."

All my friends, thought Nat happily over and over as she went to sleep that night. *I've made it to the top!*

Which meant – there was only one way left to go.

Down.

CHAPTER SEVENTEEN

• • • •

MONDAY MORNING AND SHINY NEW CELEBRITY Nat was in the playground hanging around on the outskirts of a bunch of chattering popular girls. She wasn't in the Flora Marling inner circle, obvs, but she was flipping close. She was at least now being allowed to talk to them!

The conversation wasn't brilliant, thought Nat as the girls babbled on about boys she didn't care about and TV shows she didn't watch, but she went along with it anyway, smiling and nodding and hoping it would get better.

She found herself wondering where Penny was, but when she'd tried to talk to Penny earlier she'd said she had some last-minute homework to do and had disappeared off to the library.

Darius was nowhere to be seen either, which wasn't especially unusual as Darius liked jumping out and scaring people. She remembered he had said at the weekend he was plotting something hilarious to liven up everyone's boring Monday. She looked around the playground for him hopefully.

Just then a shy little Year 7 girl asked Nat to sign her English rough book and mumbled something about Nat being "awesome and funny" while Nat pretended she hated the fuss. She pretended it VERY LOUDLY to make sure the other girls heard.

I'm definitely on my way to the Flora Marling inner circle, she thought, scribbling:

To Shoniqua,
Peace and love,
Nat the Normal Girl.

But then she saw the familiar scruffy little figure of her best friend being marched into school, surrounded by SIX teachers.

That's bad, she thought. The more teachers carting you off, the more in trouble you were; that was the rule. The previous record was five, held by none other than Oswald Bagley.

"You spelled 'Shoniqqua' wrong," said Shoniqqua sulkily. "It's got two Qs."

"Whatever," said Nat, watching Darius anxiously.

"Do it again," demanded the little girl.

"I'm busy," said Nat, breaking away from her to investigate. "Go away."

But Shoniqqua wasn't giving up. "You're rude and rubbish and you're not even properly famous," she shouted very loudly. All the kids nearby turned to stare.

"Shush," said Nat. "Get lost."

"You're being horrid. Debbie Melon from *Buckfast Manor* on the telly spelled my name right and my dad says she's got a brain like a peanut."

The girl was barring Nat's way. Nat saw Darius and his escort go into school. She desperately wanted to catch them up.

"Gimme the book and I'll do it again," said Nat.

"I don't want it now," shouted Shoniqqua. "I don't need your stinky name in my book."

Nat winced, glancing over at the popular girls and hoping they hadn't heard. *Fickle, this fame game*, she thought as she nudged her way past Shoniqqua and entered the school's big double doors.

She guessed Darius would be heading to the Head's office, but the door was closed when she got there and the bell went for lessons before she could eavesdrop.

But she didn't have to wait very long to hear what happened. At lunch break she saw Oswald drive up on his noisy black motorbike. It was never nice seeing Oswald, and this time was no different. Darius got on the back and they roared off.

"Haven't you heard?" said Penny when Nat asked her. "He's been suspended again. It's the third time this term. It's a school record."

Nat immediately went to find Miss Hunny. When she saw her in the corridor Nat thought she looked a bit cross.

"Is it true, Miss?"

Miss Hunny knew immediately what she meant. She nodded.

"Most teachers want to get rid of him, I know. And most pupils. And most of the people who live anywhere near the school too. But you were supposed to be on his side."

"I am," said Miss Hunny. "But he really did it this time."

"But he's been working ever so hard at the ugly pets' home – doesn't that count for anything? He was only selling the banned pop to raise money for it."

"He hasn't been suspended for selling the pop," said Miss Hunny, looking around furtively. "No one knew about that."

"Forget what I just said," said Nat.

"He's been suspended for releasing rats in the staff room."

"What did he do that for?" asked Nat.

"It's interesting that your first question wasn't, 'Why do we think it was Darius who did it?'"

"Ummm…" said Nat.

"He did it because it's apparently hilarious to watch Miss Austen and Miss Eyre stand on chairs holding up their skirts while shrieking like baboons," said Miss Hunny.

"Not funny at all," said Nat, biting her lip.

"No," said Miss Hunny, biting hers.

"So," added Nat, "how DO you know it was him?"

"Because the rats all had the wrong number of eyes, legs or tails. They were obviously from the ugly pets' home."

Oooops, thought Nat.

Miss Hunny smiled sadly. "Of course, the worst of it is all the teachers now think it's my fault for suggesting he should work there. They say it was a stupid idea and bound to end in disaster." She sighed.

"That's not fair," said Nat.

"Thanks," said Miss Hunny, smiling.

"I mean, it's fair they think it was a stupid idea," Nat continued. "It was a stupid idea. Darius, loose with wild animals? What were you thinking?"

"Thanks," said Miss Hunny again, in a different tone of voice.

"But Darius really is trying to be good. He's even trying to save the ugly pets' home from being closed down."

"Well, maybe if he can show that he can do good by saving the pets' home it might just save him from getting expelled," said Miss Hunny. "But I'm afraid there's nothing I can do for now. Anyway, maybe it'll do you good to get away from him for a while."

Nat got away from Darius for precisely four more hours. When she arrived home with Dad there he was, sitting on the doorstep with his little duffel bag at his feet.

"Hello, Darius," said Dad, casually letting

him in. "Hungry?"

"Starving," said Darius brightly. "Oh, Oswald says he can't be expected to look after me while I'm off school, but as you're a layabout with no job you won't mind."

"Did he say that?" asked Dad.

"Taking out the bad words, yeah," said Darius.

"Well, I think it's great that you're here," said Dad, "because it means we can plan Nat's big event on Saturday and how to make her even more famous!"

"What big event?" said Nat suspiciously.

"Great," said Darius, grinning. "Which bedroom's mine?"

CHAPTER EIGHTEEN

. . . .

A S IT TURNED OUT, THEY DIDN'T HAVE TO WAIT till Saturday, as early the next morning Nat got a text from her new (and definitely totally genuine) friend Julia Pryde saying that Nat was now... A POP STAR.

For a few seconds, staring at the text in bed, Nat felt sick. She was so used to being teased, she just thought: *This is it, I'm back to being laughed at again.* She felt even worse when more texts bonged in, more of her new friends telling her the same thing.

"Oi, Buttface," shouted Darius through the wall. "You can't sing."

She'd almost forgotten he was staying. Then he made some noises that very much reminded her. She ignored them and plucked up the courage to click the link her friends had sent her.

A band called 'The Nut Jobs' had taken the words from Nat's 'Can't you be normal' video and put it into a song. It was a pretty terrible song – the sort of song they play around the pool at the kind of holiday resorts Mum would never take the family to.

Beep-beep-beep went the song, for ages, without any words. Then something that sounded like a car alarm went off with a great *whoop*, followed by a horrible deep thudding like giant knicker elastic being twanged.

And finally, the shouty vocals came in.

I am a nutter, do you want some?

Repeated lots of times.

Then there was a lot of bragging. The singer was apparently a rather terrific kind of guy.

And finally, Nat heard herself say:

Can't you be normal? Norm – norm – can't you be normal?

Then the whole racket repeated itself, endlessly. It was truly, spectacularly, teeth-grindingly awful.

Nat loved it.

She rushed out of bed to play it to Dad, who was in the kitchen sleepily reading the paper. He said it was great and everything, but could she please turn it off now as it was giving him a nosebleed.

Nat was buzzing about being in a pop song. She even tried to fit the Dog into her schoolbag because she'd seen pictures of pop stars with little dogs in their handbags. But a big hairy farty mutt hanging out of her satchel and chewing her maths book wasn't quite the same, she realised, so she left the Dog with Dad in the Atomic Dustbin and actually skipped through the school gates cheerfully.

"Oh, hello, Nathalia, it's our own little

Beyoncé, is it?" said the familiar snide voice of Miss Eyre, who was on playground duty. Miss Austen, who as usual was standing next to her, sniggered.

But even they couldn't ruin Nat's day. Nat just had to listen for ten minutes while Miss Austen told her the school didn't need any prima donnas floating about like they owned the place. Then she handed her a bit of paper and asked Nat to get her the autograph of the lead singer of 'The Nut Jobs'.

"There's no special treatment for celebrities at this school," she said with an unpleasant wink.

When she'd gone, Nat saw that the bit of paper was actually next week's history test answers. *I'm beginning to see why people like being famous*, thought Nat.

In fact, Nat had the best day at school ever. Even better than the day Darius nailed up the staff room door and they missed a maths test.

Everyone wanted to sit next to her. And everyone told her how much they'd always really really liked her. It was brilliant. The only person who didn't want to be super-friends with her was Penny, but Nat decided that Penny was just jealous, and would come round eventually.

Even Bad News Nan couldn't put a dampener on Nat's mood that night. She had heard the nutter song on the radio and had come round to give Nat A TERRIBLE WARNING ABOUT POP-STAR FAME.

"I'm surprised you heard the song, Mum," Dad said as he handed over the biscuit tin. "You hate modern music. You've been saying you hate modern music since I was a kid and you made me turn *Top of the Pops* off the television."

"I don't like it if it's a racket and you can't tell what they're saying," said Bad News Nan, dropping her dentures in the biscuit tin again. "There's enough shouting and cursing in the world already. I can get all that down the bingo on pension day."

She flicked the crumbs out of her false teeth and put them back in. "I heard the song at the hairdresser's. I didn't need my hair doing, but I saw Gertie Dingle under the dryer and I've been meaning to talk to her for ages so I popped in. I was talking to her for twenty minutes before I put my glasses on and realised it wasn't Gertie after all; it was a Bulgarian woman called Borislava."

Nat and Dad both developed a glazed expression as Bad News Nan rambled on. It was a big tin of biscuits so they knew they were in for a long one.

"She was very nice, didn't speak a word of English, but it didn't matter. We had a lovely chat until she suddenly stood up and ran out of the hairdresser's with her curlers still in. Must be the fashion in Bulgaria."

"Did you like the song, Nan?" said Nat, hoping to hurry the story along.

"It was horrible," said Nan. "Which I suppose must mean it's good these days."

"Thanks," said Nat.

"But stop interrupting or I'll never get to my story," said Nan. "It turns out, Alan's daughter's friend was a pop star. It did not end well."

"Alan?" asked Dad weakly.

"You know Alan. Alan. My friend Gertie's daughter's cousin's friend Alan. You do know Alan, he always asks about *you*."

"Oh, OK," said Dad. "How is Alan?"

"He's dead," said Bad News Nan.

Nat put her head on the table.

"Never mind about Alan," said Bad News Nan. "I'm not talking about him, it's his daughter's friend I was telling you about. The pop star. Now, what WAS her name?"

"It doesn't matter," said Nat. "Please tell me what happened."

"Oooh it was terrible," said Bad News Nan.

"Really?" said Nat, sounding not in the least surprised.

"Being a famous pop star killed her stone dead," said Bad News Nan. She turned to Dad. "Do you know you can blend custard?"

"Why did being a famous pop star kill her, Nan?" asked Nat, suddenly slightly worried.

"She was the singer in a band on this big cruise ship. Biggest one ever, it was. Unsinkable, they said. Then it hit an iceberg and that was the end of her."

There was a long pause.

Then Dad said: "Do you mean the *Titanic*, Mum?"

"That's the one."

"That sank over a hundred years ago, Nan," said Nat.

"Rubbish. I saw the film on telly last Christmas. It was in colour. They didn't have telly back then, let alone colour."

"I promise I won't get a job as a pop star on a cruise ship anywhere near icebergs, Nan," said Nat, deciding she could risk a bit of pop-star fame, after all.

"That's all I wanted to hear," said Bad News Nan. "Sensible girl, not letting fame go to your head. What time's tea?"

CHAPTER NINETEEN

. . . .

RIDING HIGH WITH HER NEW-FOUND POP FAME, Nat had one of the best weeks ever, ending with the 'big event' that Dad and Darius had been planning that Saturday evening.

Nat the Normal Girl had been asked to turn on some new lights in the local park. Mum told her that it was high time she did something useful with her fame. "A lot of people will be listening to you," said Mum. "Make sure you say something important."

So Nat had spent the day working hard on her

speech. It started off with the ugly pets, but as she got more into it, it got grander and grander. She called it 'Girls are the light of the world'. She thought it was ace.

Dad gave her lots of jokes to put in, and better yet, Mum crossed them all out.

Nat got butterflies in her stomach when they arrived at the park and saw that tons of people had already turned up to see the lights. They were squashed into Mum's tiny red car because Mum wouldn't be seen dead in the Atomic Dustbin.

"I'm a bit nervous about this," Nat admitted to Dad as Mum parked the car.

"Don't worry, your mum's perfectly good at parking," said Dad.

"No, the speech!" said Nat.

"Oh, that! You'll be fine. Your speech is only five minutes long," Dad said. "The average military dictator can bang on for six hours and everyone in the audience has to grin and bear it."

"Why are you talking about military dictators, you daft lump?" asked Mum. "That's not helpful;

it's not like she knows any."

Dad looked at Mum in a way that made Nat giggle.

"Very funny," said Mum. "I'll deal with you when we get home."

"Firing squad, probably," said Dad. Mum laughed and punched him on the arm as they all tumbled out of the little car.

Nat was so nervous she didn't even notice that she'd left her speech on the back seat.

When they got to the big fountain in the centre of the park they saw Darius.

"I reckon half the town's turned up for this," he said. "And they'll all be looking at YOU, Buttface."

"I'm only doing it for the animals," said Nat loudly, so Mum could hear. "Fame is only good when you use it to do good things," she added.

"Yeah, right," sniggered Darius. "That and getting loads of cash and friends and free stuff."

"Mmm, what's that?" said Dad, sniffing the

air. The vans that sold hot snacks were arriving. Dad trotted off in search of food.

"Are you our little celebrity?" came a booming voice that made Nat jump.

A tremendously fat man in a loud check suit and a gold pocket watch was holding out a pudgy hand. Nat took it and wished she hadn't. It was like being gripped by wet sausages.

A thin woman with a face like a Grand National winner stood at his side, forcing a smile.

"Parks is the name, parks is my game," boomed the man. "I run the park – and my name is – Mr PARKS."

He obviously found this hilarious. He laughed until his whole body shook.

"Now you, young lady," said the woman. "We only know you as Nat the Normal Girl. We can't introduce you like that. What's your last name?"

"Bumole," said Darius with relish.

"Remove this cheeky Herbert from my park immediately," said Mr Parks.

"My name is Bew-mole-ay," mumbled Nat.

"Oh dear," said the lady. "We'll stick with Nat the Normal Girl. You're due on stage in five minutes."

She pointed to a raised platform. Nat gulped nervously.

The woman was still talking. "Mr Parks will introduce you, then your agent tells me you want to say a few words before you turn on the lights."

"Agent?" said Nat.

"Yes, agent," said Mr Parks. "We had an email from a Mr Elvis Greed Bugatti."

Nat glared at Darius.

"I'm assuming he's American with a name like that," said Mr Parks, impressed. "Very Hollywood."

"He's not American," said Nat. "I'm not even sure he's human."

"He must be foreign," insisted the woman, "on account of all the spelling mistakes in the email."

"And he says you want to talk about soup,"

said Mr Parks. "Which is fine, I suppose, but there's no room for a cookery demonstration."

"It stands for Save Our Ugly Pets' Home," said Nat, feeling like an idiot. "Only the H is silent."

"Next year we'll get someone off *The X Factor*," Mr Parks muttered to his companion.

Nat's attention was suddenly drawn to a hulking figure nearby. She recognised the black leather clothes and big bushy beard immediately.

It was Oswald Bagley. She shuddered.

"Oi, Elvis," she said to Darius. "I didn't know Oswald liked fairy lights."

"He doesn't," said Darius, "he's working for Fat Pete, the man who runs the bacon sandwich van."

"I can't see Oswald frying bacon with an apron and a little white hat on," giggled Nat.

"Nah, he's here 'cos 'Tony Four Cheeses' has turned up."

"Tony who?" asked Nat.

"Tony Four Cheeses. He runs the pizza van. Him and Fat Pete hate each other. So Oswald's gonna bash anyone who buys a pizza."

"And that's a job, is it?" said Nat, folding her arms.

"More of a hobby, really," said Darius.

"Nice pizzas, these," said Dad, stuffing his face with a cheesy slice.

"Eat it, quick," said Nat, ramming it in Dad's mouth as fast as she could before Oswald spotted him.

"Mmmf," said Dad. "Hot hot hot!"

Mr Parks turned to Nat. "Let's get you on the cherry picker," he said brightly.

"What's a cherry picker?" she asked.

"Just stand on the little platform," said Mr Parks, guiding her to the stage. Next to the stage was a big ugly crane that Nat guessed was used to put up the lights.

"You'd think they could have moved the stupid crane out of the way," she said to Darius. "It's not very attractive. And it's going to block some people's view of me."

"I thought you didn't care about being

famous," said Darius.

"I'm thinking of the animals!" snapped Nat. "The more people see me, the more ugly little animals we save. Don't you care about anything except yourself?"

"Know what?" said Darius. "I was gonna tell you what a cherry picker is. But I'm not going to now."

Nat was tempted to throttle it out of him, but there was a blast of music from the sound system that nearly blew her head off.

The show was about to begin.

And no one who was there would ever forget it.

CHAPTER TWENTY

....

THE DICTIONARY SAYS THAT A 'CHERRY PICKER' is a basket on a crane. It lifts workmen high in the air so they can do things like, for example, picking cherries, or cutting high branches.

(Or, as Nat was about to find out, it's a basket you cling on to, shrieking in sheer terror as it lifts you high into the air to turn on the town lights.)

Things started to go wrong even before she stepped into the basket. As she stepped on to the stage, she tugged Dad's sleeve.

"Where's my speech, Dad?"

Dad patted his trousers in the way he did when

he didn't want to give her money for a magazine in the corner shop. "It must be in the car," he said. "Do you need it right now?"

"Of course I need it right now, Dad, you spanner. I'm going to give my speech right now. When else do you think I would need it? Tomorrow? Next week? Halfway through double geography? When I'm in the bath?"

A few camera flashlights went off in Nat's general direction. People were starting to gather in front of the stage.

"You shouldn't screw up your face in fury like that," said Dad calmly. "It spoils your looks."

"If you don't fetch her speech in the next ten seconds I'm going to spoil your looks," said Mum. Dad hopped off the stage and sprinted to the car.

"Be back in a sec," he shouted. "Just entertain the crowd."

"How?"

"Do your catchphrase or your pop song or your funny dance." Dad was almost out of sight.

"No way," shouted Nat after him. "I'm giving a serious speech about how we should all save the ugly pets' home. Then, if I have time, I might do a bit about how girls can light up the world the way these lights light up the park."

Nat watched nervously as a scuffle broke out in the crowd. Mum was looking at her watch and tapping her foot impatiently. Darius had disappeared. Dad was still nowhere to be seen.

"Is something on fire?" said Mr Parks, standing on tiptoe. Smoke wafted over the stage. "Oh dear, it looks like one of the vans selling food has caught alight."

"Is it Fat Tony's pizza van, by any remote chance?" asked Nat.

"I think it is," said Mr Parks. "How did you know that?"

"Lucky guess," said Nat.

"Come on, Nat," said Mum. "Your father must have got lost. Let's not delay – it's time to shine."

Nat gulped.

"You'll be fine without the speech," said Mum. "Just remember the important things and speak from your heart and everyone will love you. Just don't take too long about it."

She turned to Mr Parks. "We're ready," she said.

Mr Parks breathed a sigh of relief and led Nat into a little yellow basket next to the crane. He handed her a microphone and a big red button.

"When you get to the top, say a few words, then press this button to turn the lights on," he said.

"What do you mean 'when you get to the top'?" said Nat nervously. "What top? Where am I going?"

"Hold on tight," said Mr Parks. Nat heard a mechanical noise behind her and the basket started shaking.

"I don't like it, Mum," she said.

"Look at me. Remember, Nathalia, you're my daughter," said Mum. Nat looked at Mum's firm, confident face and felt better.

"You're right," said Nat, glowing inside a little. "And like my mum, I can do anything."

"That's my girl," said Mum.

"Hey ho and up she rises!" shouted Mr Parks.

But I'm also Dad's daughter, thought Nat, *and like my dad, I get everything WRONG …*

The crane groaned, the arm stretched, and to Nat's horror, she found herself hoisted…

Up in the air.

CHAPTER TWENTY-ONE

• • • •

"AAAAAGH!" YELLED NAT, AS THE BASKET rose into the dark sky, swaying violently. She closed her eyes for what seemed like ages and concentrated on trying not to be sick. Then she heard the crowd burst into applause and that gave her the confidence to open her eyes and peek out.

But they were only clapping because Fat Tony was giving away burned slices of pizza for free.

Eventually, Nat thought of Mum's confident face and looked around, breathing deeply to stop her heart beating so fast. The cherry picker had now stopped, arm extended to its full height. The little stage below seemed miles away.

She could see the tops of the dark trees. The whole town was spread out, glowing orange under her feet. She could even see Mum's little red car. And there was Dad, struggling to fit in through the tiny door.

Too many pork pies, she thought. *He looks stuck. No wonder he didn't bring me my speech in time.*

Of course, the speech! She took a deep breath and began talking.

"Ladies and gentlemen," she began, "boys and girls, welcome to the illuminations." But her words were whipped away by the wind.

"You need to turn the microphone on, Buttface," said Darius.

"EEEEK!" shouted Nat, not realising Darius was in the basket too. Her squeal almost broke the mic, which Darius had switched on at that moment, deafening the crowd.

The speakers onstage shrieked and howled as Nat's voice thundered throughout the park.

"WHAT THE HECK ARE YOU DOING IN HERE, YOU UTTER CHIMP? AND DON'T CALL ME BUTTFACE!" shouted Nat.

"You do realise the microphone's on now, don't you?" said Darius.

Nat went white. She looked at the crowd, terrified they might have heard her horrible nickname, which was only slightly less embarrassing than her REAL name. But she saw, with a massive sigh of relief, that everyone still had their hands over their ears from her deafening scream. No one had heard. She was safe. For now.

But Darius isn't safe, she thought. She snatched the microphone from him, turned it off, and began hitting him with it.

"Gerroff," said Darius. "I only came up here to help you."

"I'll deal with you later," said Nat, then turned

on the microphone and addressed the crowd.

She tried to remember her beautifully written speech. She had been very pleased with it. It was all about kindness and helping poor unfortunate creatures, but now, the only poor unfortunate creature she could think of was herself. And the crowd below didn't seem in the mood to be kind to anyone.

She looked down and saw Dad running, exhausted, on to the stage, waving her speech. He tripped over some wires and fell flat on his face.

Fat lot of good you are now, she thought. Stupid Dad.

Her mind had gone totally blank. She couldn't think of a single word to say. Then, out of the dark, Mum's clear voice rang out.

"This is your moment, Nathalia. Take it and remember what fame is for."

She didn't need her speech. She knew what to say.

"People of the town, the quality of mercy is

not sprained," she began. She'd read that phrase somewhere and wasn't sure what it meant, but she reckoned it sounded brilliant.

"Girls are the light of the world, just like these lights tonight are the lights of the, um, park. And I want these lights to light the way to your heart. And when you find your heart, have a good look round in there and see if you can find a place for the little animals."

She was on a roll. She was on top of the world. She was actually *enjoying* this. She didn't need her stupid speech.

"They might be ugly and violent, but that's not their fault. They might smell a bit and leave nasty stains all over the house, but so does my nan and we still love her. So please help us save Porter Ogden's Ugly Pets' Home. If you do, I promise to do my funny dance and everything."

Her voice was choked with emotion. "Bless you all, goodly townsfolk, and thank you for listening."

She gave a very theatrical bow.

"What?" said a voice in the crowd.

"Speak up, we can't hear you," said another.

"Your microphone's not on," shouted a third.

"Whoops, sorry," shouted Dad. "I think I must have pulled a wire out when I tripped over. Sorry, love. Can you say all that again?"

He plugged a wire back in, there was a howl of feedback and Nat's furious answer came booming back at a volume you normally only get by sticking your head in a jet engine.

"DAD, YOU HAVE TOTALLY RUINED MY LIFE, YET AGAIN."

"That's not how your speech starts," said Dad, peering at it. "You've written something about mercy."

"This is rubbish!" shouted yet another voice from the darkness.

Dad grabbed another mic from the stage and addressed the crowd.

"THAT'S MY DAUGHTER UP THERE AND SHE'S ONLY DOING THIS TO SAVE THE PORTER OGDEN UGLY PETS'

HOME. SHE DOESN'T EVEN LIKE BEING FAMOUS, NOT REALLY. SHE'S A LOVELY LITTLE GIRL AND YOU SHOULD BE NICE TO HER. SHE'S NAT THE NORMAL GIRL, FROM THOSE FUNNY VIDEOS."

"Oh, I like HER," said a woman in the crowd. "Can she do the little dance?"

"COURSE SHE'LL DO THE DANCE," said Dad. Nat scowled.

"BUT I DON'T THINK OF HER AS A NORMAL GIRL," continued Dad, who was enjoying being onstage now. "I DON'T THINK SHE'S NORMAL AT ALL. WOULD A *NORMAL* GIRL DO ALL THIS JUST TO SAVE HORRIBLE PETS?"

He had the crowd's attention now.

"NASTY, ROTTEN PETS. PETS THAT MOST SANE PEOPLE WOULD WANT TO PUT IN A SACK WITH BRICKS AND LOB IN A LAKE?"

"You should stop now," said Mum.

"HONESTLY, THEY ARE VILE," continued

Dad. "ONE OF THEM NEARLY TOOK MY FACE OFF."

"Ivor!" snapped Mum. Dad jumped.

"ANYWAY," said Dad, changing the subject, "TO YOU SHE'S NAT THE NORMAL GIRL; TO ME SHE'S JUST NATHALIA, NATHALIA BEW—"

Nat KNEW what he was going to say. Quick as a flash she pressed the red button and the park blazed into all its second-hand illumination glory. "I DECLARE THE LIGHTS – ARE ON!"

There was a gasp and then a cheer. It was... like a fairy wonderland. It was actually, properly *beautiful*.

"I hadn't finished," said Dad, but Mum had already taken the microphone off him.

Mr Parks threw another switch and rockets shot up in the air, showering the crowd with rainbow-coloured sparks.

Nat turned to Darius, amazed.

"I GOT AWAY WITH IT," she said.

"Shut up," said Darius.

"DON'T INTERRUPT," said Nat. "THIS WAS BRILLIANT. THE LIGHTS ARE GREAT, I WAS SUPER FAB EVEN IF NO ONE HEARD ME, AND BEST OF ALL, MY STUPID DAD DIDN'T TELL EVERYONE MY REAL NAME IS NATHALIA BUMOLÉ!"

There was a roar of laughter from the crowd.

"I was just gonna say your microphone was on again," said Darius.

"BUM'OLE! BUM'OLE!" came the chant from the crowd.

Nat slumped to the bottom of the cherry-picker basket.

CHAPTER TWENTY-TWO

••••

"O N THE BRIGHT SIDE, YOU'RE PROBABLY EVEN more famous now, which is good for trying to save the pets," said Dad the next morning at the kitchen table.

"Shut up, Ivor," said Mum, who was eating a healthy bowl of muesli and looking enviously at Dad's massive bacon sandwich. "She doesn't want to be famous at all, can't you see that?"

Nat was looking online at the 'breaking news' section of the local newspaper with a stony face.

"The photographer must have had a very long

lens to get that angry expression on your face from all the way up there," said Dad, still trying to cheer her up. "Apart from your face, it's a lovely picture, with you all lit up by the lights and fireworks. Can you print that out?"

"Sure, Dad, shall I print out the headline too?" said Nat.

VIDEO STAR HITS BUM NOTE! laughed the headline.

"There's loads of stuff online about what went on last night," said Nat. "But it's all about either my rubbish speech or my stupid name, or some leather-clad bearded mystery man's 'reign of cheesy-slice terror'."

"It was quite eventful," agreed Dad, looking at Mum's raised eyebrows. It was the sort of eventful she did not approve of.

"There's NOTHING about the pets' home and that's mostly the only reason I did it," moaned Nat. "Why does everything you're involved in end up being so completely utterly EMBARRASSING?"

"Oh look," said Dad, reading over her shoulder, "there's a nice quote here from your agent, Elvis Greed Bugatti. I didn't know you had another agent."

"It's Darius, you moron," said Nat, slamming her laptop lid down. And slamming her head on it for good measure. She wasn't feeling well and last night's humiliation was the final straw.

"Being famous is HORRIBLE," said Nat, sneezing violently. "I've had enough of it. It's given me a cold. I'm going to bed and don't wake me up until everyone's forgotten all about me."

Nat's cold got worse as the day went on. She was snuffly and bunged up and her head ached and her throat felt red raw. Her temperature went up as her spirits went down. She was even too sick to enjoy Dad getting a proper telling-off from Mum.

She didn't dare turn on her phone. She knew it would be full of texts making fun of her stupid name. She had a thoroughly miserable day and when finally, drowsy with cold remedy, she drifted off into a sniffly sleep, she prayed she would wake up totally unknown again.

The next day was Monday and Nat was way too sick to go to school. She tried to cheer herself up by calling Dad up and down the stairs about a hundred times. Mum had to go to work, but Nat didn't think she'd mind Dad suffering for his crimes.

By the afternoon, she was feeling a bit better. Dad had brought her a cup of tea (nice) and a bottle of cough medicine (nasty). *That sums up my life,* she thought. *Nasty always follows nice.*

"Go away, you've ruined my life, and I'm not even joking," she said snottily.

"I see you're on the mend," Dad said cheerfully, "and you'll feel even better when you see what the postman's brought you."

Nat dragged herself out of bed with shaky legs and trudged downstairs in her onesie. What the postman had brought was a sack full of letters and parcels.

"Fan mail," said Darius, who was sitting on the sofa eating beans from a tin. "Can you believe it?"

"I don't want fan mail, I don't want fans, I don't want to be famous," sniffed Nat, plonking herself down on the sofa. "It's horrid and embarrassing and awful. Send them all back."

She looked at some of the bigger parcels for a while. She was tempted... but no, she had made up her mind, she had had enough...

She stood up, turned her back on it all, and marched upstairs.

Two minutes later she marched back down, writhing with indecision.

"Do it, do it, dooo it!" chanted Darius.

"I shouldn't," said Nat, touching a letter briefly, as if it was hot. "Besides, they might be saying mean things." Her fingers picked at the Sellotape of a big box. "Celebrities get nasty letters as well as nice ones."

She looked at the labels. "And I'm certainly not opening anything addressed to the 'Bum Girl'," she said decisively.

"Probably best, now you mention it," said Dad. "But the others should be OK."

"Just get on with it," said Darius, who had already spread bean juice on most of the packages.

"Hang on," said Nat. "How did these people know where I live?"

"They don't know where you live – I'm not totally daft," said Dad. "But this is the address for my new Talent Agency. It's on the website Darius made."

"I'm just ace," said Darius modestly.

"Talent Agency?" said Nat.

"Bumolé and Bagley. Sounds good, doesn't it?"

"It sounds terrible."

"That's what I said," said Darius. "I said it should be 'Bagley and Bumolé'."

"Mum is going to kill you."

"Possibly. But your mum's in a meeting in Milan or Madrid or somewhere beginning with 'M'."

"Is it definitely miles away?"

"Miles and miles."

They all stared at the mail for a while.

Nat knew Dad loved packages. They reminded him of Christmas, which Dad also loved. Mum said that was just because it was the only time of year he got paid.

"I should open one box," said Nat. "Just so I know what I'm sending back."

"Good idea," said Dad.

Nat opened the first box and out tumbled a whole load of really nice tops.

"That's lame," said Darius.

"OMG!" said Nat. "Are these for me?"

"They don't suit the colour of my eyes so I guess so," joked Dad, holding one up. It was full of holes and said:

I'm a rebel. What against? What have you got?

Another one, equally ripped, said:

Be yourself because nobody else can be.

And a third had:

This is what cool looks like. Deal with it.

"Oh, they're all torn," said Dad. "I'll definitely send them back now."

"They're supposed to be torn," said Nat. Then she spotted a tiny label on each of them.

DBGG.

She almost squealed in delight.

"Dad Dad Dad Dad, they're the new tops from Dinky Blue, Girl Guru, *Rebellion – Be Yourself* range!" she gabbled. "Everyone wants these."

"There's a note in the box," said Dad, rummaging about. "Oh, it's from her publicity people. Let's see, they say you can keep them as long as you wear them every time you get photographed. And say how great they are, and what good value for money."

"They *are* good value for money," cackled Nat, her cold and her shame forgotten. "I won't be fibbing. They're free!"

She ripped open another box.

"Get in!"

"Is it ray guns of doom?" said Darius

hopefully.

A delicious sweet smell filled the living room.

"Bath bombs, my fave! Ooh and candles and body washes and scrubs, plus moisturisers, conditioners, moisturising conditioners, conditioning moisturisers, lip balms, hand creams, nail creams and, urgh, spot cream – cheek! – and an organic sponge."

Darius, now totally bored, hopped off the sofa and walked off in disgust to play with the Dog.

"Who's it from?" said Dad.

"Splash, obviously."

"Splash?"

"Dad, you are so old. This is their whole new range of *Kid in a sweetie shop* products. It's all good enough to eat." She read a card. "I'm right, it's from Splash. It says: 'Please use them all, with our compliments.' Thanks, I will. Dad, can you run me a bath, please?"

"I take it you're keeping everything then," said Dad.

"Maybe I was being selfish," said Nat,

opening more parcels. "I was only thinking about myself and how horrid it is being famous – and it really is very very horrid – but I was forgetting about the poor pets. And Darius, of course."

"Can't forget Darius," agreed Dad.

"So just maybe I should put up with being famous until I save the— whoa, a new phone! And these trainers are lush!" Nat settled down to read a bunch of letters from little girls telling her how funny and great she was.

Yup, I'm definitely doing this for the pets, she thought. "Oi, Dad," she shouted, "is my bath ready yet? If I'm gonna say how brilliant my new bath bombs are, I have to try them out. It wouldn't be professional otherwise."

Nat settled down in her big steamy bath feeling that just maybe she'd be able to face everyone at school tomorrow. *OK*, she thought, sliding into the bubbles, *so the thing at the park didn't go according to plan, and everyone's having a good giggle at my name AGAIN, and yes, the voice-over went badly and of course there's that video of me with a bird in my hair and another one of me jumping up and down shouting about being normal, but as someone said in a movie once: Fame costs and this is where you start paying.*

She stretched out in the delicious-smelling water, thick with *Splash*'s finest, newest and gloopiest bath products.

It's a tough job, she thought, *but someone's got to do it.*

She tipped some more bath foam under the hot tap, and bunged another couple of bath bombs in for good measure.

She put her head back on a free bath pillow and closed her eyes. *I hope the horrible ugly pets appreciate all my hard work*, she thought, totally relaxing. Until she noticed... that her head, hands and feet were no longer poking out of a nice hot bath, they were poking out of a pink, rock-hard, bath-sized bath bomb.

All the lovely chemicals she'd put in the tub
had mixed and reacted and then *fused together*
in a sort of evil mud, trapping her in a massive
block of sweet-smelling concrete.

"DAD!" Nat yelled, wriggling helplessly. She
was lying at a funny angle and her arms and legs
had gone to sleep. She realised with horror that
she wasn't able to break free. She was stuck fast!

"DAD!"

Dad opened the door.

"Are you all ri—" he began. Then saw her and burst out laughing.

"Don't you dare laugh!" she yelled. "It's definitely not in any way funny."

"I'm not laughing," laughed Dad, stuffing a hanky in his mouth to stifle his giggles. "But you have to admit, it's a bit funny."

"Get me out."

He tapped the rock.

"How much did you put in?"

"Some. All. I don't know. Do something."

"That is properly solid," he said, scraping at it with his nail.

"I do know it's solid, Dad."

"I'll probably need a hammer and chisel."

"You are not going to hammer-and-chisel me out. I'm not a statue," said Nat crossly.

"I don't want to hurt you. We should call in the experts."

"The experts? In getting girls out of bath bombs? Who are the experts in that?"

Twenty minutes later she got her answer as a couple of firemen entered the bathroom and started laughing uncontrollably.

"I've got toes out of taps and fingers out of plug-holes, but in thirty years of being a fireman, I've never seen anything like this," said one of them as he prised Nat out of her rocky prison.

"Get that camera away from me!" shrieked Nat, now draped in towels, as she saw a lens on a fireman's helmet.

"Health and safety, I'm afraid," said the fireman. "We have to video everything these days. It's OK, it won't end up on the news."

It didn't. It ended up somewhere worse.

CHAPTER TWENTY-THREE

· · · ·

"AT LEAST NO ONE CAN SEE ANYTHING RUDE—you're all covered up by the giant solid bath bomb," said Dad the next day.

Somehow, the fire brigade's video had found its way on to the Internet.

The video was called *Another Normal Day for Normal Girl*. It featured blurry images of her trapped in what looked like a giant pink sausage, along with the hysterical firemen rolling around on the bathroom floor.

It had already got over a million hits. Nat

reckoned she had felt each hit personally, like little pinpricks. She spent the day pretending she had still got a terrible cold. She was hoping to stretch out her illness until she was eighteen when she could leave school and get a job in a town where no one had ever heard of her.

But she couldn't avoid returning to school forever and the next day she knew she'd have to face the music. As Nat approached the school gates, she fully expected everyone to snigger at her stupid embarrassing name or to laugh at the toe-curlingly awful bath bomb video.

Which they all did, obviously.

But it was even worse than that.

From snatches of conversation she overheard in corridors, in the playground, in the cloakroom or the loos, it became clear that most of the school now thought Nat was just *showing off*.

"She just wants attention, all the time," said one girl.

"Yawn. Another day, another Nathalia video," said another.

And the worst of all:

"I liked her early videos, when she was funny."

Nat was just praying that, even though her popularity seemed to be fizzling out, she was still famous enough for Flora Marling to let her come to her mega secret birthday pool party sleepover on Saturday.

"I'm more famous than ever now," Nat said to Darius that evening. She wanted to put her head on the kitchen table in misery, but it wasn't her kitchen table she was sitting at, it was the greasy one in Porter Ogden's pets' home, and there were very few surfaces there that anyone would wish to touch.

"Yeah, it's good," said Darius, eating dog biscuits with his mouth open.

"No, it's TERRIBLE," said Nat. "It would have been bad enough facing everyone at school after the park disaster, but now it's 'Oh look, here comes the Bath Bomb Bumhole'."

"That would be a brilliant hashtag," said

Darius as Nat threw a tin of cat food at his head.

"And I don't understand girls. First they liked me because I was a little bit famous and now they don't because I'm *too famous.*"

"They'll like you again if you get even more famous," said Dad. "That's how fame works."

"Shut up," said Nat. "Can't you see I'm really confused?"

"Oh, and next time you make a dead funny video without me," continued Darius, "talk about the pets' home, Buttface. We're saving it, remember?"

"Yes, I remember the pets' home; I'm sitting in the pets' home," snapped Nat. "Actually," she said, reaching down, "what AM I sitting in?" She looked at her hand and pulled a face. She wiped it on Darius.

This was a crisis meeting between the directors of 'Bumole and Bagley Talent Agency' (Dad and Darius) and their most famous client (Nathalia).

The meeting was in their new office (Porter Ogden's Ugly Pets' Home). Dad decided to move the agency in case of 'possible emergencies' (Mum finding out about it and hitting the roof in rage).

"I'm not talking to either of you about it any more because you are both totally sacked," said Nathalia, sitting with her arms folded. She was ice-cold angry and her chill filled the room. She looked very much like her mother.

"Every so often, *Dad*, I think 'This is the most humiliating thing that's ever happened to me', but I'm always wrong. There's a massive list of 'most humiliating things that've ever happened to me' to choose from and I keep thinking, *No they can't get any worse*. But then they get worse."

She stood up and pointed to the video taken by the fireman. "But THIS video – this is definitely the most humiliating. And so I'm not doing anything you suggest ever ever again."

"To be fair, I didn't suggest that you put all your bath stuff in the bath in one go," mumbled Dad quietly.

"What about the pets?" said Porter Ogden, who was washing blood out of his trousers. He looked tired, worried and half-chewed. "What about the little pets?"

"Stuff the little pets," said Nat.

"Great idea," said Darius. "We could sell stuffed pets as ornaments or voodoo dolls. I say we stuff Simba first."

"She doesn't mean that sort of stuffed," said Dad. "Or do you?"

"Can either of you take anything seriously, ever?" said Nat. She looked at them and sighed. "Stupid question."

She got up, shoved her chair away roughly and stomped out into the back garden.

She needed some fresh air. Of course, what she got was less fresh and more stinky, rotten air, but still...

Ooh that's a bit ripe, she thought, sniffing the aromas from the cages and wrinkling up her nose. It was like standing downwind of Nan after Christmas dinner.

She found a patch of grass between the mud and the jungle, checked it was more green than brown, and plonked herself down. Nat could just make out the roofs of the houses nearby and she wondered if any of them had girls inside having as rubbish a time as her.

Bet they don't, she thought, picking a daisy savagely. I bet they've got *normal* families and *normal* friends.

The infamous words, 'Can't you be normal?' buzzed around her head, tormenting her, like a mosquito trapped in a sleeping bag.

She shook her head to clear the buzzing noise, then realised there was a REAL buzzing. There was a dirty great wasps' nest under a branch of a nearby tree. Nat watched as they flew backwards and forward in the late afternoon sunshine.

Even the insects here are ugly, thought Nat. *There wouldn't be butterflies or anything, would there?* A mournful howl started in the cages, followed by a sinister hissing Nat recognised as coming from the evil Simba. An old, broken slate slid off Porter Ogden's roof and smashed by the back door.

This place really is a mess, she thought. *Maybe, just maybe knocking this house down and spreading concrete all over it and building a shiny new car park isn't such a bad idea?*

Nat looked down and realised that she was absent-mindedly stroking a pathetic-looking bundle of damp, muddy fur that had crawled out of a pond. She peered at it. It was Fang, a beaver with no teeth and a flat nose. It looked like it had been chasing brick walls.

The gummy beaver sucked on her hand wetly.

"Gerroff," she said, pushing

it away. "You sound like my nan eating trifle."

Fang the useless beaver shuffled back to her and started slurping on her hand again.

Nat giggled. "That tickles," she said. "You stupid toothless beaver. What's the point of you?" The beaver made a rude noise and Nat thought that, from a certain angle, it looked like… Darius.

She sighed. Darius was also annoying and smelly and a bit pointless. And he was in trouble too. She remembered Miss Hunny saying that saving the pets' home might just save Darius from being expelled. Then she imagined him living rough on a rubbish tip with only the revolting monkey and Simba the Dreadful for company.

Maybe he'd like that, came the same voice that was trying to tell her why car parks were ace.

Yes, he probably would like it, admitted the real Nat. *But I wouldn't.*

She thought of all the times he'd stood up for her. She could walk down the darkest corridors of school and no one would dare tweak a single hair of her head, just because she was best mates with Darius Bagley.

School without Darius jumping out of cupboards or putting superglue on the toilet seats or ever finishing his epic poem *Diarrhoea* or telling the world's best jokes or helping her with her maths? Unthinkable.

Nat chuckled to herself remembering Darius overhearing the slimy Lucy Tapper from 9C make fun of Nat's 'Normal' video, then tipping a box of worms into her Spaghetti Surprise.

She remembered the grin on the little menace's face as he was hauled off to the Head's office, followed by a shrieking Lucy Tapper picking munched worms out of her braces.

Nat tried to imagine school life without him. It was quieter; it was less bonkers; it was less smelly, embarrassing, weird and revolting.

But it was rubbish.

He had to be saved.

And so did the pets' home, with all its unfit, unloved and unlovable creatures. It was the right thing to do.

She wasn't Nat the Normal Girl, or Nat the local celebrity or even Bath Bomb Bumole. She was 'The Girl Who Always Did The Right Thing, Eventually'.

That was the Nat she liked.

Even if no one at school does, she thought glumly.

She trudged back to the house, her mind made up. She was on the side of the angels. Even if the angels were really ugly angels with snotty noses, busted wings, terrible table manners and a naughty streak a mile wide.

She was going to save the flipping ugly pets' home.

AND SHE WOULD DO IT WITHOUT USING HER EMBARRASSING, RUBBISH FAME.

But she had less than a week and she didn't know where to begin.

Nearing the back door, she felt like one of those superheroes in the films Dad liked to watch. There was always the bit towards the end of the film where the superhero can't use his superpower because it's too dangerous… yet it's the only thing that can save them all!

Then she trod in something.

This never happens to Iron Man, she thought bitterly as she scraped it off her shoe.

CHAPTER TWENTY-FOUR

. . . .

"WHAT'S A DOSH-A-THON?" ASKED NAT, WALKING back into the kitchen and overhearing the strange word.

"What's that smell?" said Darius. Nat ignored him.

"We're not actually going to call it a Dosh-a-Thon," said Dad. "But basically, it's a live celebrity online pet home eviction night fundraiser," said Dad.

"Not as catchy as 'Dosh-a-Thon'," said Darius.

"We'll work on the title," said Dad, writing something on a pad. "The plan is, we just raise the money to buy the land from the council so the developers can't get it. Simple."

"A million quid?" said Porter Ogden. He had the sort of tone of voice Nat recognised. It was mostly total disbelief with a note of 'Are you taking the mickey?' on top. It was the way Mum said: "HOW fast did you say I was going, officer?" to traffic policemen.

"Be sensible," continued Porter Ogden. *That's rich, coming from you*, thought Nat, *bearing in mind your idea of a great life is to share your home with several hundred of the world's most horrible creatures.* "No one is going to give you a million quid."

"We don't need one person to give you a million quid," said Dad.

"No," said Darius. "We need one million people to give you one quid."

"How are you going to find one million people to give me a quid?" said Mr Ogden.

Dad tapped the laptop.

"Cyber-crime?" said Mr Ogden hopefully.

"Of course not," said Dad.

"Actually, that's not a bad idea," whispered Darius.

"No," said Dad. "Stick to plan A. We're doing a live, twenty-four-hour charity fundraiser! On the inter cyber-space web, from this very house! It'll be great."

He turned to Mr Ogden. "We'll have famous guests, we'll do films about the animals, we'll interview you and your neighbours – actually, no, let's not interview your neighbours, they all hate you – and everyone donates a pound and you're saved!"

"The best of it is – we've already got our live host – Nat the bath-bomb... er, I mean, Nat the Normal Girl!"

"You what?" said Nat.

"Your last video got *two million* hits. OK, it was a little bit horribly embarrassing, but people liked it. You get recognised, you get free stuff, you get fan letters from mad people. That makes you a star. Good causes need stars and we need you."

Nat sighed dramatically, mostly for effect. "OK, I'll do it!"

Darius and Dad whooped and high-fived.

"When is it?" she asked.

"This Saturday," said Dad. "It's the last possible day we can do it before the council start bulldozing next week."

Nat's blood turned cold. "Um. Actually, I can't. I promised Mum I wouldn't do any more videos or anything else to make me famous. Sorry."

"Nothing to do with the fact that Saturday night is Flora stupid Marling's stupid party then?" said Darius.

"Oh, I'd totally forgotten about that!" fibbed Nat, thinking *I'll get you later, Bagley.*

"I know you don't want to be famous any more, but we can't do it without you, love," said Dad.

There was a long pause. Even Simba stopped munching on some poor, slower creature to listen.

"Yeah, you can!" said Nat, leaping up excitedly. She had just come up with A BRILLIANT AND AWESOME PLAN.

"I know people who LIKE being famous," she said. "They just love it. The sort of people who can get a million hits before breakfast. In fact, Vernon the Cereal Guy gets *ten* million hits for just eating his breakfast, but that's because he eats it through his nose."

"What are you talking about?" said Dad.

"It's probably the fumes from the sewers," said Porter Ogden. "With all the animals, the air gets so foul sometimes I start babbling and seeing things too."

"There's Pretty Penny, who teaches you how to put make-up on. She gets twenty million new followers when she opens a packet of eyeshadow. There's Hashtag Naturally Fab who shows you what face to pull when you're taking selfies –

she's great. Oh, and Lip Balm Cutie, Vintage Veronica, and Sweary Mary, who tells you how many times people say rude words in a film. Hilarious."

"Who *are* these horrible people?" said Dad. "I don't want you being friends with any of them."

But Darius understood what Nat was on about, and had some ideas of his own:

"Don't forget Doom Ninja Pete, the man who blows things up. His last vlog got fifty million. Mind you, he did explode a camel."

"Vlog?" said Porter Ogden, confused.

"Video blog," said Dad, proud of himself for vaguely understanding something modern. "It's the language of us young people."

"I understand the word *video*…" said Porter Ogden, still confused.

Nat was properly excited now. "And I've finally got an excuse to message Dinky Blue, Girl Guru!" she said, clapping her hands.

"I know these are words," said Mr Ogden. "I just don't know what they mean."

"Basically, there are tons of people who are mega-famous online," Nat explained. "Much more famous than me."

"If you say so, but I've never heard of them," said Porter Ogden.

"It's a different famous," explained Dad. "It's like a secret famous."

"I think your family is madder than my family," said Porter Ogden. "And my grandfather went over Niagara Falls in a barrel."

"Why?" asked Dad.

"Well, he wasn't going to go over *without* one, was he?"

"Anyway," said Nat, trying to get them back on track, "the point is that the web is stuffed with loads and loads of people who are super way more famous than Nat the Normal Girl could ever be. They love being famous. I'll just get one of *them* to do it."

CHAPTER TWENTY-FIVE

• • • •

THAT NIGHT, NAT SENT MESSAGES TO ALL her favourite vloggers, asking for help. She started with the boring girl who just filmed herself taking new things out of boxes, and went all the way up to the awesome Girl Guru herself, Dinky Blue.

Darius even made her send a message to the awful Doom Ninja Pete.

"How long is Darius actually suspended for?" Dad shouted through the loo door that night.

"I dunno," said Nat, who was standing on the

landing. "Anyway, I'm not talking to you when you're on the loo, it's disgusting."

"I have to talk to you on the loo – someone's put superglue on the seat," shouted Dad. "I say *someone*, but it doesn't take Judge Judy to work out who's guilty."

Nat couldn't stop herself giggling.

Dad was quite cross by the time he came downstairs, but fortunately Darius had worked out how to unscramble the movie channels on telly and get Dad's favourite films for free, so instead of shouting, Dad got himself a pork pie out of the fridge and settled down to watch *Aliens vs Cowboys* on a big soft cushion instead.

Mum came home later that night and asked Nat how she was getting on with not being famous any more.

"Did you follow my advice and get rid of all those silly gifts you were sent?" Mum said as they tucked into their Chinese takeaway.

"I did," admitted Nat, crunching on a spring roll. "But it made things worse. People follow me around expecting presents now."

"I meant give them away to charity, not to your silly new friends," said Mum with a sigh. "I don't want you turning into Mimsy."

"Mum!" said Nat, horrified that Mum could even think of comparing her to the horrible spoiled daughter of Dad's friend Posh Barry. "You know Mimsy is the very last person in the world that I want to be."

"I know that," said Mum gently, giving Nat a hug. "Apart from any of your nan's friends, of course. You definitely don't want to be one of them."

Nat giggled. Bad News Nan's friends all seemed to catch revolting diseases that Nan liked to describe during Sunday dinner. Sometimes she brought photos. Dad said she was just making sure there'd be tons of leftovers.

"I thought being famous might make me popular," admitted Nat. She could talk about this stuff to Mum. "But now Penny hardly speaks to me, the other girls talk behind my back and I don't even know if I'm still invited to Flora Marling's secret birthday pool party sleepover any more as she hasn't spoken to me for ages."

"Have you asked her?" said Mum.

"You don't just go up to Flora Marling and talk to her!" said Nat. "You have to wait for her to talk to you. Anyway, I wish I'd never done that stupid dance video in the first place," said Nat. "I'll be famous forever now."

"Oh no, fame never lasts," said Mum. "There's a ton of old pop stars who work in burger vans, or models who stack the shelves at Aldi. The man who brings the sandwiches to my office used to have his own TV series. And now he's getting told off for bringing me white bread when I plainly told him I wanted wholemeal."

"You're not really making me feel better here, Mum," said Nat.

Darius and the Dog started a howling competition in the garden.

"How long is he suspended for?" asked Mum.

"Dunno," said Nat. "Can I tell you a secret,

though? It's great having Darius here. Did you hear he superglued—?"

"Yes, I heard."

"And have you seen his trick where he—?"

"He's not a pet," said Mum sternly.

"I know. He's not even house-trained," giggled Nat.

"But seriously, Nat," said Mum, "maybe it's time to start winding this whole fame thing down and get things back to…"

"Normal?" Nat finished for her, and they both laughed.

No one at school believed Nat when she said she didn't want to be famous any more. It didn't matter how many times she said she was fed up with being stared, pointed and laughed at – she still got stared, pointed and laughed at.

And now everyone expected her to like it.

At lunch that day, Nat went to track down Penny, who she was pretty sure had been avoiding her. But even Penny didn't have much sympathy.

"Everyone's just waiting to see what mad stuff you get up to next," explained Penny with a thin smile.

"I want to do something important – I'm trying to save this pets' home," said Nat for the seventh time that day, "but everyone just wants me to act like a fool."

"At least people think you're funny," said Penny, examining her lunch for anything edible. "It could be worse."

Nat felt a cold shiver run down her spine. "Funny?" she said. "I *hate* people laughing at me."

"I thought you'd be used to it by now, especially with *your* dad."

"Thanks," said Nat.

"I'm just saying, no one's ever gonna take you seriously when you're famous for being…" Penny hunted for the right expression.

"Famous for being *what*?" growled Nat.

But before Penny could reply, a heavenly scent drifted across Nat's table as Flora Marling floated by, with her friends/adoring slaves following behind.

Flora smiled at Nat. "Hey, I've been meaning to say – I was in the park last week when you turned on the lights – hilarious, like always. You are *totes hilarious*."

"Mmm, totes hilarious. That's the expression I was looking for," said Penny under her breath.

"And then that bath bomb video – wow, you are so brave. That's edgy comedy."

"I like edgy," squeaked Nat.

"And now you're doing the whole 'Oh, I don't wanna be famous, stop looking at me' thing. That's SOOOO clever."

"I actually mean it," said Nat.

"Course you do," said Flora. "Still on for Saturday?"

"Yes, please," said Nat too quickly and then, desperately trying to play it cool, added, "you know, if I'm not doing something... edgy."

"You know what you sound like?" said Penny, after Flora had gone.

Yup, I sound like a girl who's going to Flora Marling's mega secret pool party sleepover, thought Nat happily.

But then another voice in her head, that sounded a bit like Darius's, said: "*No, you sound like a spanner.*"

"It's not my fault," said Nat with a sigh. "I really am trying not to be famous any more. I'm sick of it."

"Well, you should have thought of that before you started your ugly scrabble for celebrity," said Penny, pushing back her chair.

"My ugly what?" said Nat, annoyed.

"You've lost your grip on reality. Instead your life's becoming like some terrible reality show," said Penny, storming off.

Back home later, Nat was telling Darius about her row with Penny.

"She said my life was like a reality show. Can you believe it?" said Nat, still offended.

"Your life's too boring to be a reality show,"

said Darius. "If you were a bounty hunter or a pirate or a masked wrestler or a champion hot-dog eater, THEN it might be worth watching. But it's boring boring boring."

"No, those reality shows generally are quite boring," said Nat.

Nat noticed a strange look come over Darius's face.

It was strange because it was unusual.

It was Darius *thinking*.

"What?" said Nat.

"Nothing," said Darius with a grin. "You get any of those stupid vloggers to help us?"

"Not yet," muttered Nat.

It wasn't quite true – she had got one reply, from Doom Ninja Pete. It wasn't what she'd hoped for either. His message said:

Hey Nat the Normal, or shd I call u bumhole bath bomb? :) :)
Would <3 to help out with ugly pets.
Which ones wd u like me to blow up?

Darius flicked a bogey at the wall expertly. "Well as you're still the most famous person we've got, you'll have to do the Dosh-a-Thon if you can't find someone else."

"I'm sure someone will get back to me. They're just very busy people," said Nat.

"Oh yeah, takes ages to watch movies or put make-up on or film yourself putting Ricicles up your nose," said Darius.

"I'm going to my room," said Nat huffily. "If you have anything useful to say, put it on a postcard. And address it to my bum."

With that she walked off, feeling quite pleased with her parting shot.

Behind her, Darius smiled.

CHAPTER TWENTY-SIX

••••

THE NEXT MORNING, NAT CAME DOWNSTAIRS
and caught Darius in the living room
looking at her phone.

She snatched it off him.

"Why are you looking up Penny Posnitch's
number?" she asked, reading the screen.

"She wanted help with her maths," said
Darius.

"Fibber. I'm the only person who knows
you're good at maths. You spend most lessons
hanging upside down in the book cupboard.

What are you up to?"

Darius grinned. "Nothing," he said, walking out of the room.

Nat had quite a good day at school, surprisingly. She thought her fame might be wearing off at last because she was only teased about it seven times.

She spent her breaks chatting with the other chosen few who were going to Flora Marling's mega awesome secret pool party sleepover.

This must be what it's like to actually BE normal, she thought as they discussed what shoes and tops they were going to wear. It was a bit dull, but it didn't really matter as long as it meant she was still a little bit popular.

Every so often she caught sight of Penny, hovering about in the background, playing with her phone.

Poor girl, thought Nat with a sigh. *I used to be on the outside too. Maybe I should try and include her?* But when she caught Penny's eye and beckoned to her, Penny shuffled away guiltily.

When Nat got home that evening, she overheard Darius on the phone in the kitchen.

"The footage you sent is all rubbish," Darius was saying. "It's all shoes and tops and blah blah blah. I'm falling asleep. No one's gonna watch this."

Nat paused outside the kitchen door. She loved a good eavesdrop. She wondered what the heck he was talking about.

"I can't take out the boring bits," said Darius. "If I take out the boring bits I haven't got a show, cos it's *all* boring bits."

Nat leaned forward too far and accidentally opened the door with her head.

Darius threw the phone into the sink.

"What are you up to?" said Nat suspiciously.

"Talking to a vlogger about the Dosh-a-Thon," said Darius quickly.

"Good luck with that," said Nat. "No one's

got back to me. It's almost as if they don't care."

She left Darius to it and went upstairs. She had important decisions to make. About tops and shoes. As she was going upstairs, she thought she heard Darius say: "Fine, get more people involved if that's what it takes."

Huh, maybe he's found someone to do the Dosh-a-Thon after all, thought Nat hopefully as she closed the door to her room.

That night Nat dreamed that Darius came into her room and pinched her mobile phone. It seemed ever so real, right up until the moment he turned into a monkey and swung out of the room on the lightshade.

When she actually woke up the next morning, her phone was still there. Although it was unplugged and she was sure she'd left it charging…

The next day at school was not normal. It was not boring.

You couldn't make this stuff up, thought Nat,

when she finally got away.

Of course, she was wrong. All day, everyone around her seemed to be running or shouting or pointing. It was worse than the WAKE UP!!!! days.

At break, everything she said was either:

"AWESOME!"

Or:

"AMAZEBALLS, NATHALIA!"

Or:

"TOTALLY HURTFUL, I CAN'T BELIEVE YOU SAID THAT TO ME. I'LL NEVER FORGIVE YOU EVER!"

It was just as bad in class as out. Even something as simple as handing out French vocab sheets turned into a drama.

"It's always me who has to do that, Miss," wailed Julia Pryde, leaving her desk and standing next to Nat for no apparent reason. "Isn't that right, Nathalia?"

Nat shrugged. "I dunno," she said. She was still trying to sneakily finish her French homework and was rather hoping no one would look at her.

Julia hopped up and down in a tantrum until Madame Hérisson led her out to the sick room and put a damp towel on her head.

At the end of the day, Nat was in a hurry to leave school and get to a SOUPH meeting at the ugly pets' home. But every time she tried to get through the school gates, one of her classmates grabbed her and started yelling hysterically.

They all seemed to have the most astonishing personal problems, all of which urgently needed Nat's advice to sort things out.

Apparently:

Bettie Flipchart's dad had just been framed for a robbery he didn't commit.

Trudi Button's uncle bashed his head playing cricket and now thinks he's the Supreme Commander of the People's Democratic Republic of Wolverhampton.

Erin Nasal was having a crisis because her mum had grown a beard and now wanted to be called Derek.

And Susan Plug had just found out that she had been cloned and now didn't know which one of her was real.

It was INSANE.

CHAPTER TWENTY-SEVEN

• • • •

T HERE WAS A DIGGER PARKED OUTSIDE PORTER Ogden's pets' home. It had PROPERTY OF BLACK TOWER ESTATES written on it. Some cheery fellow had put a note in the digger window. It said, simply.

SOON.

"Nice people," said Nat.

"I think we should get 'em back," said Darius, coming out of the house and indicating two tins of bright yellow paint. "I found these in your shed."

247

"I remember those tins," said Nat. "The council were painting double yellow lines in front of the house and Mum, um—" She stopped. She didn't want to grass Mum up. Darius just laughed.

"Your mum is awesome," he said.

"What do you want to do with the paint?" said Nat impatiently.

"We're going to tell the truth about these horrible developers."

"OK, but I'm not doing anything that makes me more famous."

"It's the opposite of famous," said Darius. He handed her a black woolly balaclava hood. "This will completely cover your face."

"Where did you get this?" said Nat.

"There's loads of them lying about my house," said Darius. "Try it on."

"Urgh, it's full of beard hair," said Nat, muffled by the hood. "Is this Oswald's?"

"It suits you," said Darius. "Whoever you are in there. Now get up there and write: 'Evil developers go home. Save the animals'."

"Why do I have to do it?" said Nat, nervously holding a pot of paint and a brush. Darius grunted as he put up a big ladder against the Black Tower Estates sign.

"Because you can spell," he said.

"You can definitely spell some of it," said Nat. "'Evil', for one thing."

"I'll just hide in the bushes and make sure no one's coming," said Darius. "Up you go. Make sure you use your best handwriting."

Nat noticed he had Dad's mobile phone in his hand. "Why are you pointing Dad's phone at me?"

"I'm not. I'm just looking after it for him. Hurry up, someone might be coming," said Darius quickly.

"It's really hard to see in this balaclava," complained Nat, climbing up the first few rungs. The ladder creaked against the sign.

"Yeah, that's what Oswald says," said Darius.

"You sure my dad's not looking?" said Nat.

"Nah, I asked him to put a flea collar on Simba," said Darius. "That'll keep him busy."

From inside the house, Nat thought she could hear Dad saying something along the lines of: "Aaaagh! Nice kitty, good kit— Waaaah that stings, you little… not the face, not the face!"

Yup, *pretty busy*, she thought.

She balanced her tin of bright yellow paint on the top of the stepladder.

"What am I writing again?" shouted Nat.

"Evil developers go home. Save the animals," shouted Darius.

She started painting.

"You're too quiet. Tell me how you're feeling," shouted Darius.

"Why?"

"Just so I get an idea of how dangerous and exciting it is," said Darius, who was looking at the phone for some reason. "I don't want to miss out. Don't mumble."

"Yes, it's exciting and dangerous. Now lemme concentrate."

She got as far as 'Evil develop' when she stopped.

"I can't reach any further," she said. "I'll come down and you'll have to move the ladder."

"Why did you write it so big?"

"So people could see it, dog breath."

"She's kidding, I haven't really got dog breath," said Darius. "It's actually minty fresh."

"Who are you talking to?" said Nat as she reached the ground.

"Myself," said Darius.

Nat looked around, but couldn't see anyone. "Move the ladder," she said, "and hurry up."

"Don't be so bossy, I'm in charge."

"You are so not in charge, chimpy."

"Don't call me chimpy, Buttface."

"Don't call me Buttface, yellow face."

"I haven't got a— Blaaagh!"

He said "blaaagh" because Nat slapped him in the face with the wet paintbrush.

He hopped up and down and tried to grab the brush, but Nat was taller than him and held it above his head, giggling. Every so often she slapped him round the face with it again.

"STOPPIT STOPPIT STOPPIT!" yelled Darius.

"No –" slap – "no –" slap – "no," said/slapped Nat.

Darius was now backed against the ladder with Nat walloping him over and over again.

"And while I'm at it," she said, enjoying herself, "this is for putting that Normal video online in the first place and this is for getting me involved with the horrible pets' home and THIS is for the cherry picker and THIS is for the bath

bomb, even though that wasn't your fault, and this is for fame being so rubbish and this is for luck!"

"This is all wrong," spluttered Darius, knocking into the ladder.

Nat whipped off her uncomfortable, scratchy balaclava.

"What's all wrong?" she said, properly baffled.

Then the tin of yellow paint fell off the top of the ladder – right on to her head. She was utterly, totally, stickily, plastered.

"Ah, now it's right," said Darius.

Nat was so shocked she couldn't move, not until the paint had trickled right down into her new trainers.

"You look like you've popped the world's biggest spot," laughed Darius.

Nat ran inside the house, squelching all the way. *At least no one will ever see THIS*, she thought (wrongly, as it turned out).

It's quite difficult to get a bit of paint out of your hair. It's incredibly difficult to get out half a tin of industrial, super-hard-wearing, double-yellow paint-of-doom.

Amazingly, Mr Ogden proved to be a bit of a star. From deep in a cupboard he dug out a jam jar of some weird gloop he'd made himself.

"It's the only thing that's ever got my hands clean after a day mucking out the cages," he said, slapping a big handful on her head. "If I tell you what it's made of, you'll never let me put it on you. But it's all natural ingredients."

"That makes it worse," she wailed, rushing upstairs to wash her hair.

Incredibly, within ten minutes she was down again. There wasn't a trace of paint *anywhere*.

"Told you," said Mr Ogden, proudly.

"Worked out all right in the end," said Dad, driving home with sticking plasters all over his face. He looked at Nat, who still couldn't believe she was clean.

"Yeah," said Darius with a sly smile, "it worked out very well."

He patted his pocket, where there was a mobile-phone-shaped lump.

CHAPTER TWENTY-EIGHT

• • • •

THE NEXT DAY AT SCHOOL WAS EVEN MORE BONKERS than the day before.

It started with a scrap on the football pitch between two Year 7 boys. Nat was among the cheerful crowd that watched Artie Spangler mash Bert Hickey's face into the grass.

Eventually there was more grass in Bert's mouth than on the halfway line, and the fight fizzled out. But on her way to the first lesson, Nat was grabbed by Julia Pryde, who said, very loudly, "OMG, Nat, that was AWESOME. You know they were fighting over you?"

"What?" said Nat, who wasn't really listening as she'd just remembered she still hadn't done her French homework. She'd spent all the previous night choosing tops to wear to Flora Marling's ace mega secret pool party sleepover instead.

"They said there's a space to be your boyfriend now Darius is out of the way," said Julia.

"Darius isn't my boyfriend! And now I've got a bit of sick in my mouth, thanks very much," said Nat, wondering why Julia was fiddling with her phone like that.

"You're playing it cool, but you must be burning up inside," prompted Julia.

"No, but I will be later – it's chilli for lunch," joked Nat.

"HA HA HA HAAA!" laughed Julia, way too loudly. "Oh that's a good one, he'll definitely use that." She turned to a girl next to her, who nodded.

Nat was utterly perplexed, but didn't have time to ask what the flip was going on because at that moment the bell went for lessons.

But lessons didn't get much more normal. In English, Miss Hunny made everyone write a poem called:

What my heart needs.

Nat pulled a face. *That is so soppy*, she thought. She spent half an hour coming up with nothing and then realised what Darius would do. She giggled to herself and wrote:

What my fart needs.

Then she wrote a big list, including sprouts, cabbage, baked beans and fizzy pop. She was trying to think of a rhyme for 'broccoli' when Miss Hunny said:

"Time's up, let's hear them. Nathalia, we'll start with you."

Nat scrunched up her fart poem.

"Dog ate it, Miss," she said.

Miss Hunny called her to the front and

handed her a poem.

"Just read this out," she whispered. "And try to look out of the window into the sunlight as much as possible."

"The light makes me squint, Miss," said Nat.

"Do as you're told," said Miss Hunny, "it's for your own good."

Nat read the rubbish poem and tried not to throw up. It went:

My heart needs…
Sunlight on roses
And fresh fluffy kittens
The laugh of a child
When I'm kissing his nosey
Mum-knitted mittens
And the call of the wild
Hugs for the world
And you – by my side.

When Nat finished she saw the whole class were dabbing their faces with hankies.

"So moving, Nathalia," said Miss Hunny. "So, so moving."

"It's like I'm living in some kind of mad soap opera," said Nat to Penny as they were leaving school.

"Don't be silly," said Penny quickly. She kept looking around for some reason. "That's just like you, that is. A soap opera, starring you, of course."

"I didn't mean that," said Nat. "I just mean everyone's acting funny."

"So I'm funny, am I?" said Penny, throwing her schoolbag on the floor. "Is that all I am to you, a clown?"

"Are you actually talking to me? Why do you keep looking round?" said Nat, confused.

"I don't know if I can take this any more!" wailed Penny theatrically. "It's hurting too much inside, you know?" She stood perfectly still for a moment, the only movement her trembling lip.

My house is less barmy than this school, thought Nat, walking off and leaving Penny to it. *Which is super-weird, cos my house has got Dad and Darius Bagley in it.*

Nat was very glad it was the weekend at last.

CHAPTER TWENTY-NINE

••••

SATURDAY MORNING – THE DAY OF THE PARTY – finally arrived.

Nat felt she now had the perfect excuse NOT to go to the Dosh-a-Thon at the ugly pets' home that night.

"But you're the most famous person we know," said Dad as they tucked into their bacon and eggs. "No one else we've asked has even replied."

"I'm sorry, Dad," said Nat, "I would like to help, but I've had a whole week without being online, or opening a shop, or having a make-over, or being sent so much as a free chocolate biscuit or anything. I reckon I am now officially NOT FAMOUS."

She glugged her tea happily.

"Which means I'm no good to you, even if I wanted to help. Which means I can now go to the greatest party of all time, ever."

"You really want to go to this party, don't you?" said Dad. "I do get it. You might not believe this, but I wasn't very popular at school."

No, I believe it, thought Nat, and gave him a hug.

Darius padded into her room later and asked if she'd changed her mind.

"Nope," she said. "My famous days are way behind me, like when someone from a boy band goes solo."

She chuckled. She was on good form today.

"Anyway, you must know someone a bit famous who can help," said Nat. "There's famous people everywhere these days."

"I do know someone," said Darius slyly. "Someone with their own reality show that's watched by over a million people every day."

"Well, they'd be perfect. Get them to do it."

"They won't because they're going to a stupid party instead."

"Well, you know celebrities," said Nat lightly, "shallow shallow shallow. They love a party. I know that because I used to be one. Now get lost, I'm going to get changed."

Nat made Dad park the horrible Atomic Dustbin half a mile from Flora Marling's house.

"I'm not taking any chances that her sister will see us in the van. She's even more awesome than Flora. She's a model."

"You're a model."

"Dad, I did it once and ended up with half a ton of litter, a bird and a mad cat in my hair. That's not like being on the cover of *She's So Gorgeous* magazine five times."

The Marlings' house was the last house on a very leafy street. It was white and modern and shaped like a big glass box. It was lit up with soft coloured lighting and it reminded Nat of a fish tank at the dentist's.

"I'm going to come in to make sure there's a responsible adult around," said Dad, walking Nat to the door.

"Why? Mum leaves me alone with you all the time," said Nat.

"Ha ha. Well I hope you have fun tonight. And don't worry about us, we'll work something out."

Nat felt a pang of guilt. "I wouldn't be much help to you anyway," she said. "I'm not famous any more, remember?"

"You just have a nice time. Oh, you know Penny's coming round to help out?"

"Yeah, I know. She sent me a text saying she'd rather be with the things that are 'ugly on the outside but beautiful on the inside'. Very funny, I thought, but it's not like she was even invited."

They rang the doorbell. "Don't embarrass me," said Nat, but then gasped as the door was opened by the most beautiful woman she'd ever seen. Possibly the most beautiful woman in the world ever.

"Oh, it's the Normal Girl!" breathed the vision at the door with a huge white smile. "And you must be Mister Bew-mow-lay."

"Blurble," said Dad, staring at Flora's sister. Nat kicked him.

"Don't worry, we'll take good care of her. We're just going to watch a few videos and have an early night," said Chloe Marling with a yawn.

"In that case Nathalia might as well come and help save the horrible pets?" said Dad, recovering. But Chloe Marling was already pulling Nat inside.

"See you tomorrow," she said, closing the door.

Chloe led Nat by the hand through the house. It was beautiful. Everything was white and there was no mess anywhere. Nat couldn't believe anyone lived there.

It was very quiet though. Nat had a horrible feeling that maybe Chloe was telling the truth and there wasn't a party after all.

"The party's through here," said Chloe, opening a door at the back of the house. Steam and light and noise blasted through.

"Welcome to the pool house," said Chloe.

Nat stepped through into...

Wonderland.

CHAPTER THIRTY

· · · ·

THE POOL HOUSE WAS LONG AND SLEEKLY COVERED in slender wooden planks. Its sloping glass roof had already steamed up. It was full of girls in swimming cossies standing around chatting and looking cool.

Nat wondered why none of them were in the pool. She could see a huge pink inflatable dolphin that was floating in the pool and she was already desperate to jump on it.

A huge stereo system was blasting out Princess Boo's new hit. There was a table with huge plates full of strawberries and marshmallows, and next to it was the biggest, gloopiest chocolate fountain that Nat had ever seen.

Nat decided there and then that eating a chocolate strawberry floating on a pink dolphin in Flora Marling's pool house would be without a doubt the single best thing that could or would ever happen to her.

Two soft hands covered her eyes. "Guess who," said Flora Marling.

"Blurble," said Nat, just like Dad.

"You made it," said Flora, taking both of Nat's hands. "Chloe, you should have invited Nat's dad in, he's hilarious."

"I hope your pool's heated, because everyone here's so cool there's gonna be an iceberg," gabbled Nat before she could stop herself. "OMG that was cheesy, wasn't it?" she stammered, making it way worse.

"I told you she's a riot," said Flora, smiling. "She just doesn't care WHAT she says."

No, I do, I really do, thought Nat, in agony.

"All these girls are so stiff, no one's even in the pool," said Flora. "I mean, who can resist a giant pink dolphin?"

"Not me!" said Nat.

"Oh good, I knew you'd get the party started," said Flora, sauntering off. "Gotta go, mingling, mingling."

"You can put Flora's present on that table over there," said Chloe, pointing to a table groaning with parcels.

"Present?" said Nat, going hot and cold at the same time.

"Yeah, I couldn't think what to get her either," said Chloe. "I mean, it's not every day you become a teenager, is it?"

Nat walked over to the present table as cheerfully as Anne Boleyn walking to the chopping block.

She had forgotten to buy a present!

She had been so excited by the words, 'Flora Marling's mega secret birthday pool party' that she had totally forgotten the little word that came in the middle – birthday.

She desperately rummaged about in her overnight bag to see if there was anything she could give Flora. *She doesn't want a pair of your pants, Nathalia*, she thought hopelessly.

In times of great stress, Nat did two things. First, panic.

I'm doomed, I'm doomed, she thought, panicking.

The second thing she did was to stop panicking and think: *What would Darius do?*

Two seconds later, she whipped off a label from a present and wrote:

Happy birthday Flora,
Love Nat.

Then she went off to get changed. A few minutes later, Nat emerged in her swimsuit and said hi to Julia Pryde and the other girls she knew from school. As per usual they were talking about boys and clothes.

Nat played along for a while, smiling and laughing in the right places. But she soon got bored and wandered off to help herself to a marshmallow. She dunked it in the fountain and looked around. She saw that most of the girls were fiddling awkwardly with their phones.

"What are they all doing?" Nat asked no one in particular.

"They're probably telling everyone who's NOT here that they ARE here," laughed Flora, floating up to Nat. "Instead of just enjoying themselves."

Flora was wearing the prettiest dress in the history of the world. "Totally," said Nat, spilling chocolate all over her fingers.

"If they're not on their phones they're always online," said Flora, "and that's so *weak*. It's like they're all trying to get five minutes of fame. Oh –" she put her hand over her mouth – "no offence."

"Totally," said Nat. *Oh, come on, think of another word, Buttface*, she yelled at herself silently.

"I don't go online much," said Flora. "It's not

272

real, you know?"

"Totally," said Nat. *AAARGH.*

"I mean, if you're going to talk to someone, look them in the eyes and talk to them."

"Totally," said Nat. *Shut up, you moron.*

"It means way more when you talk in real life."

"Totally," said Nat. *I give up.*

"You're funny," said Flora, and drifted off for another real conversation.

Nat decided that talking wasn't her strong point so she thought she'd slip into the pool, given everyone else seemed to be too busy on their phones or posing around the edges to have any actual fun.

She couldn't believe there was still no one on the dolphin.

There is now, she thought, paddling over to it and scrabbling on, holding her chocolate marshmallow above her head.

Done it, I win, ha, she thought, relaxing on the dolphin's wide back.

This lasted five minutes and twenty-eight seconds.

Because that was when Hettie Putin, the girl who always won the shot-putt on sports day, decided to do a massive dive-bomb into the pool.

It was a poor choice and might have been massively caused by the fact that she had just glugged a can of something she'd been saving for the party.

That's right, the very last can of WAKE UP!!!! pop.

"Look at me, I can fly!" yelled the normally quiet and reserved Hettie. She took a massive run up and launched herself towards the water.

Turned out she couldn't fly, but she could hit the front of the dolphin with the force of a cannonball. There was a massive squeaky, farty noise as little Nat was pinged right off the dolphin, out of the pool and up into the air.

"WAAAH, HELLLP!" shouted Nat as kids scattered beneath her.

"Get out of the way!" she yelled as she came down on the table full of tasty party food.

Squelch! She landed right in the sticky marshmallows, which at least broke her fall.

Whoop! went the chocolate fountain, shooting up at the other end of the table and spurting dark chocolate liquid high in the air.

Oh what a surprise, was the last thought that went through Nat's mind, *here comes choc-ageddon.*

Gloop! went the chocolate, as it started to come down.

Here we go, thought Nat, splayed out in the squashed marshmallows. *Here comes a gallon of chocolate. With any luck the fountain will hit me on the head and I'll be knocked out until everyone's gone home.*

Nothing happened. Only a huge gasp from all the kids around the pool.

Funny, thought Nat, finally realising the fountain hadn't landed on her. *It's always me that gets covered in stuff. Well, result.*

The chocolate didn't land on Nat.

It landed on Flora Marling and the world's prettiest dress.

CHAPTER THIRTY-ONE

. . . .

FLORA STOOD, STILL AS A FROZEN STATUE, ABSOLUTELY covered from head to toe. She looked like a melted Christmas tree decoration, a chocolate angel put too near the fire.

Until that moment, Nat had thought the worst thing that could possibly happen was for the chocolate to land all over her, in front of all these other girls. But as she watched the gooey brown mess drop steadily off Flora Marling's perfect nose, she realised this was far, far worse.

No one said anything for an entire five long,

awful doom-laden seconds.

And then Flora Marling did the coolest thing of all time ever.

She laughed!

She threw her chocolate-covered tresses back and said:

"Chocolate's on me, guys."

Everyone cheered and started dipping their strawberries and marshmallows on her.

Eventually, Nat scraped herself off the table and walked up to Flora, head hung in shame.

"I'm so SO sorry," she said.

"It's a party, it's not meant to be serious," laughed Flora.

"You are awesome," Nat blurted out. "However famous I became, I would NEVER have been as cool as you."

Whoops, she thought, *did I say that out loud? Well I just proved my point. NOT cool.*

Unfortunately, though, all the other girls weren't quite as cool as Flora Marling was about choc-ageddon. As they crowded round Flora, they twittered and gossiped, whispering about Nat.

"Who does she think she is?" said one.

"She ALWAYS has to be the centre of attention," muttered another.

Nat, who'd had quite enough of being talked about, sighed and went to get cleaned up. She spent ages showering off the marshmallow goo in the little wet room next to the pool house. She didn't really want to come out of the shower, ever. Not for the first time recently, she wished Darius had been there.

Darius. Her heart sank as she thought about his cheerful, evil little goblin face. She'd let him down, she'd let the ugly animals down, and for what? So she could make a total spanner of herself in front of a bunch of boring girls who she didn't even like that much anyway.

Nat looked at her reflection in the bathroom mirror. She didn't much like what she saw. *It's fame that led you here*, she thought. *Well at least I can put a stop to that.*

She sighed. She knew she didn't belong in a swanky wet room in a super-posh house full of boring posers.

She belonged at a stinky ugly pets' home full of horrible drooling animals. And the horrible drooling Darius Bagley.

As she left the bathroom, Nat saw Chloe Marling in the corridor, frowning at a door that was slightly ajar.

"Hmmm," Chloe said, "no one's supposed to be in here."

She opened the door and found a small gaggle of girls, including Julia Pryde, huddled over a laptop.

"Out," said Chloe, sounding very grown up.

"We're just doing our hair," said Julia Pryde guiltily.

"Don't lie to me," said Chloe, sternly. "Now you aren't supposed to be in here, are you?"

"No, Miss," said Julia Pryde. She looked very small and young and silly.

"Now run along," said Chloe. The girls

shuffled out, casting envious glances at Nat, who was standing next to the awesome Chloe.

"Doing their hair, my foot. Just cos I'm a model now, everyone thinks I've changed into someone stupid," said Chloe.

She went over to the laptop to see what they were looking at.

"Does fame change you?" Nat blurted out, remembering she was talking to a genuinely famous person.

Chloe tapped a few keys on the laptop.

"Nah," she said. "Fame's just a magnifying glass, that's all. I've met a bunch of famous people. And I reckon if they're spanners now, they were always spanners."

Uh-oh, thought Nat.

"Which famous people have you met?" she asked, finally.

Chloe Marling reeled off a bunch of names like she was reading a shopping list.

"And you," she finished, with a smile.

"Very funny," said Nat. "I'm not famous

any more."

"You kidding? I wouldn't miss an episode of Nat the Normal Girl."

"Who? What?"

"...although I was a bit disappointed in you. About your big decision tonight."

"Wha-wha-what big decision?" said Nat, sitting on the bed and feeling the world moving from under her.

"I was hoping you were going to try and save the animal home," said Chloe.

"Animal home? How do you know about that?" said Nat, cold with fear.

Chloe's face broke into a massive smile. "OMG," she said. "You're such a great actress. OK, I'll play along. Let's pretend you don't know. I'll tell you how I know."

But even before Chloe explained, Nat realised that she DID KNOW.

She knew why everyone had been acting weird at school.

She knew why her life had turned into a

soap and why everyone around her was always playing with their phone.

She knew why Darius had locked himself away over a laptop every night.

Even before Chloe turned the screen towards her, Nat knew.

Even before she read the words:

MY NORMAL LIFE

A REALITY SHOW STARRING NAT THE NORMAL GIRL

Episode 4: A BIG DECISION!

She knew.

Her life had felt like a reality show – because it WAS a reality show!

CHAPTER THIRTY-TWO

····

"OH, WOW, THIS EPISODE IS UP TO DATE," SAID Chloe. "Look, there's you in the pool house taking the label off one of Flora's presents. Oops, naughty!"

Nat covered her eyes, and then peeked through her fingers like she was watching a horror movie. It WAS a horror movie. There she was, caught red-handed on camera (well, wobbly mobile phone footage) swiping the label.

"I hope they've got the scene with the dolphin and the chocolate fountain," said Chloe.

"Turn it off, turn it off!" wailed Nat. "Who knows about this? Does anyone actually watch it?"

"About a million people, that's all," said Chloe. "But more are tuning in every day."

Nat felt sick, but Chloe chatted on happily. "I mean, you haven't got Dinky Blue, Girl Guru viewing figures yet, but give it time."

"This is so horrible," said Nat, throwing herself full length on the bed. "My life is literally over."

"Oh, that looked great, but I haven't got a camera," said Chloe. "Do you want me to film this bit?"

"No, I do not!" yelled Nat. "I don't want to be filmed by anyone ever again for anything."

"So – you really didn't know? And you're not pleased?" said Chloe, finally understanding. "Not even a little bit?"

"No. I hate my life and now I'm going home to jump in a big hole and…"

She stopped and clenched her tiny fists in fury.

"No, I'm not," she said with a chill to her voice that Mum would have been proud of. "I'm going to the ugly pets' home."

"Oh, you are going to save them!" said Chloe. "Yay!"

"No, I'm going to kill Darius Bagley, live on air."

"I'll drive you over there!" said Chloe helpfully. "Let me get my car keys."

Nat was waiting by the front door when Flora Marling walked past her.

"I just found out about that stupid reality show," she said.

"Hilarious, isn't it?" asked Nat unhappily.

"I think they were all horrible to you. I'll be crossing some people off next year's party list." She smiled at Nat and floated off. Nat was too stunned to reply.

Porter Ogden was in the front garden of his doomed ugly pets' home, smoking a pipe. He was wearing a suit that was old but surprisingly clean.

Behind him in the house, animals howled and lights flickered.

"They didn't want me inside," he said as Nat hopped out of the car. "They said I was getting in the way and scaring off the viewers." He coughed and spat. "Now they're complaining that without the pipe smoke, it smells too bad in there. Can't win."

He ushered them through the front door, which was covered in the scratches of a thousand claws.

The kitchen had been turned into a sort of ramshackle TV studio. The boxes and crates and dirty dishes had been pushed to one side in a big heap and they'd draped an old tablecloth over them to make a backdrop.

Someone had painted 'Save the ptes' on it.

Nat guessed it was Darius.

The Dosh-a-Thon show was in full swing. Penny Posnitch was behind Dad's old video camera set up on a tripod, filming everything. Dad and Darius were sitting in front of the screen.

There were wires everywhere. Dad looked tired. There was a ukulele with only one string left unsnapped at his feet. Nat guessed he'd been trying to entertain the world for hours.

There was a monkey on Darius's shoulder, eating bits of wax out of his ear.

To one side of them rested a huge picture of a unicorn. The horn had been left blank, to be filled in as donations came in.

There was a sign on the horn reading:

Donation totaliser.
Target – one million pounds!

At the bottom was a tiny felt-pen line, showing how much had been raised so far.

It stood at £2.50.

"It's going well then," whispered Nat to Chloe sarcastically.

Penny must have heard something because she turned around. When she saw Nat, she burst into a big, relieved smile. She ran over to her.

"I knew you'd come!" she said. "It's been a disaster. Darius is up to verse 391 of his revolting poo poem, your dad played his stupid ukulele for two hours nonstop and Miss Hunny said she's coming round later to do a magic act."

Then she saw Chloe.

"Flipping heck," she said, trying to get her hair in place.

"Who's that on the screen?" said Chloe, looking at a young girl wearing too much make-up and being very intense.

Nat's mouth dropped open.

Live on the screen was none other than the biggest vlogger of them all:

Dinky Blue, Girl Guru.

And she was talking about Nat!

But not in a nice way.

"I mean, what sort of whacko person leaves these sick animals for a party?" said Dinky Blue.

"They're not sick," said Dad.

"And she's not a whacko," said Darius.

"They sure look sick. And she sure looks like

a whacko."

"You don't understand," said Dad. "I *wanted* her to go to the party. I'm glad she did."

"I don't get it. Hurry up and explain. I'm a very busy vlogger. I've got to prepare a video on how to be kind to people, even if they're not really worth being kind to."

"I'm now going to de-giblet Bagley live on air," whispered Nat. "I don't care how famous it makes me."

But Chloe grabbed her. "Wait," she said. "I wanna hear this."

"Nathalia really wanted to help these animals," said Dad. "And she doesn't want to be famous. Or at least, maybe she did for a bit, but not really. And I feel terrible about it because I put her dance video online in the first place. So that's why I didn't mind when tonight she just wanted to go to a normal party like a normal girl, not 'THE Normal Girl', if you see what I mean."

"It wasn't a very normal party," giggled Chloe.

"Yeah, right," said Dinky Blue. "EVERYONE

wants to be famous. If she doesn't want to be famous, why has she got her own reality show?"

"What reality show?" said Dad. "Darius, do you know anything about this?"

"We're losing the connection," said Darius quickly, hopping off his chair and running towards the laptop.

But before he could get there, someone jumped into his path and grabbed him. He looked up.

Right into the cold, furious eyes of the world's latest reality star – Nathalia.

CHAPTER THIRTY-THREE

....

DARIUS BROKE FREE AND MADE A RUN FOR IT. Unfortunately, he tripped over a trailing wire and went headlong into the backdrop with a huge crash. The carefully stacked boxes, crates, cages, dishes, pot, pans, garden chairs, bits of wood, pipe, tiles, buckets and other rubbish...

... all fell on top of him.

Nat dived into the pile after him. For a few moments, the two of them thrashed their way through a sea of rubbish, fur, feathers and scales as a bunch of the animals broke free and joined in the fight. The noise was tremendous.

Nat thought she'd finally got him, but found she was throttling a large one-eyed lizard. Something licked her face. She pushed it off and dived into the rubbish again.

"Get filming," she ordered Penny. "I don't mind this video going worldwide. People need to know I've got rid of this evil for good."

She saw one of Darius's scruffy trainers and pounced.

"Aaaarrgh!" he yelled.

She hauled him up. He had a dirty saucepan stuck on his head and she clanged him with a potato masher until his eyes rolled round.

"Give me one good reason why I don't carry on mashing you!" she said.

"Glark," said Darius.

"Why did you do it?" she said, mashing harder. "Why why WHY?"

"You liked being popular," he blurted out. "And you said being famous made you popular."

Nat stopped mashing.

"You wanted to be friends with the popular girls. So I tried to keep you famous. So you would stay popular. I thought you'd be happy."

There was a long, long silence, save for Simba slowly crunching the unfortunate lizard in the corner.

"OMG, Darius, you've ruined my life and that's the nicest thing anyone's ever done for me."

Chloe and Penny wiped tears from their eyes. Even Porter Ogden's wheezy cough was gentler than usual.

Dad was on the phone. He shouted: "Someone's offered us a tenner if Nat keeps mashing Darius!"

But she'd dropped the masher.

"Chimp," she said.

"Buttface," he said.

They turned to Penny, row forgotten.

"Bighead," said Penny.

"Airhead," said Nat.

Penny smiled.

"Sorry," said Nat.

"All right," said Penny.

Nat picked up the potato masher and handed it to Penny. "You can mash Darius if you like," she said.

"No, you're way better at it than me," said Penny.

"Come on then," announced Nat to the room. "Stop standing about. Let's get to work. We've got a pets' home to save!"

Just then, Mum walked in.

Nat gave her a massive hug and said: "It wasn't my fault I've been the star of my own show. I knew nothing about it, honest. I was trying not to be famous and everything…"

"What show?" said Mum.

"Forget I said anything," said Nat.

"I came here to support your father's silly fundraiser. My company are offering him a thousand pounds if he promises never to play the ukulele again."

"Is that your company or you really?"

whispered Nat. Mum grinned.

"Right, kids, let's get the show back on the road!" said Dad. "Come on, round up the animals, rebuild the set, put the camera back and stop Simba eating my foot – AAARRRGGGH!"

That night, everyone took part in the Dosh-a-Thon.

Dad set fire to his ukelele for twenty quid.

Darius got a pound for every verse of his epic poem *Diarrhoea* he could remember off the top of his head. He got five hundred and six pounds.

Porter Ogden told rude jokes that made Dad cover Nat's ears.

Penny Posnitch drew a picture of fairies on unicorns being chased by Simba and sold it for two hundred pounds.

Miss Hunny popped by and did a magic act, which was great until she went to pull a rabbit from a hat and just pulled out Simba with a bunny tail in its mouth.

Chloe Marling gave a make-up tutorial and

almost crashed the Internet.

Mum went on camera and told everyone firmly that they needed to donate – she got over ten thousand pounds in thirty seconds.

"How much more do we need to get to a million?" asked Nat sleepily, at about two in the morning.

"Nearly a million," said Darius.

"How about you?" Mum said to Nat. "You're our star."

Nat shook her head. "I'm done with fame," she said.

"Well, that's good," said Mum. "You shouldn't go looking for fame. But occasionally, just maybe, fame finds you for a reason."

There was a pause. Finally, Nat stood up. "Mum," she said, "there's something I have to do."

She walked in front of the camera.

"Hello, viewers," she said, hopping up and down, "why are you watching us? Can't you be normal?"

CHAPTER THIRTY-FOUR

• • • •

THE DOSH-A-THON MIGHT HAVE SAVED NAT'S friendships with Darius and Penny.

But it didn't save the home.

By Sunday afternoon, the money had been counted. They were still a way off from their million-pound target. Darius quickly worked out how much off:

£985,235.21p off.

It looked like the Black Tower Estates people were going to flatten the home and the sad fate of the animals – and Darius – was sealed.

But then...

On Monday morning a man in a suit from a big company came round with a chequebook to buy Porter Ogden's incredible paint cleaner. The man's daughter was a big fan of Nat's reality show and her favourite bit was the paint fight. Her father couldn't give two hoots about two silly kids chucking paint over each other, but he almost fell off his chair when he saw the cleaning gloop in action.

On Tuesday morning Porter Ogden put on his best suit, went round to the council offices and gave them the money and a right telling-off. He made sure the local news was there too. He fancied a bit of this fame thing.

He never revealed how much he got for his invention, but he also bought the house of the boss of Black Tower Estates, knocked it down and put a car park on it.

"Did you hear Chloe Marling got her own reality show?" Nat asked Darius as they were sitting in maths the following Friday.

"No, don't care," said Darius. "X is twenty-four by the way, not two hundred and six."

"Ta," said Nat.

Julia Pryde looked across at them and scowled at Nat.

"It's OK," said Nat, ignoring her. "Some people are meant to be popular, and the rest of us just aren't."

Monkey noises appeared to be coming from inside Darius's desk.

"You do know you can't actually bring King Kong to SCHOOL, right?" said Nat bossily.

"Nat," said Penny, who was sitting behind her, "wanna come to my house tomorrow? Princess Boo's got a new song out. We could do another dance video."

After all she'd been through, all she'd learned, it would have been absolutely utterly, completely bonkers for Nat to say yes.

"Yes," said Nat.

The End

Nathalia's dad has been embarrassing her since before she was born.

FOR INSTANCE, it's his fault that she has the world's worst surname and has collected more hideous nicknames than she can count on both hands AND feet. It's not easy making friends when you're (not exactly affectionately) known as Nathalia Buttface. Or worse.

And don't mention Dad's old van so full of junk that it's like a bin on wheels – and prone to do things like burst into flames in the school carpark IN FRONT OF EVERYONE IN NAT'S CLASS.

Now, finally, Nathalia has a chance to start afresh – at a new school, in a new town – but with the same old Dad. Unfortunately.

This isn't going to end well.

Most girls would be over the moon if their dad told them they were off to the South of France for the summer.

But unlike Nathalia, most people don't have the MOST EMBARRASSING DAD IN THE WORLD. Not only does his surname mean she'll be called Nathalia BUTTFACE for the rest of her life (or even longer), but he also looks RIDICULOUS in shorts, gets all pink and peely on his bald spot, and thinks speaking French means speaking in English with a stupid accent.

Maybe this holiday will be different, though. A farm in the South of France with a pool. Surely even Dad can't ruin this?

Don't bet on it!